ADVANCE PRAISE FOR *AS THE EARTH DREAMS*

"An important anthology of speculative fiction from a talented new generation of Black Canadian writers. There's great imagination at work in this book, including gardens from across history connected by a portal, a cousin who can fly, and a store where migrants sell their memories. Rich, original, and varied, this book offers visions of the future—and the past—that we really need in our troubled present."

—Larissa Lai, author of *The Tiger Flu*

"*As the Earth Dreams* is a stunning anthology of some of the most intimate and evocative speculative fiction I've read. The balance of themes, concepts, and emotion is masterful. This book is a jewel in the Canadian fantasy and science fiction landscape."

—Sonia Sulaiman, editor of *Thyme Travellers: An Anthology of Palestinian Speculative Fiction*

"The work in *As the Earth Dreams* provides the kind of literature I crave: brilliant stories that challenge and provoke, while exploring what it means to be human in fresh and interesting ways."

—Arley Sorg, literary agent and editor

AS THE EARTH DREAMS

AS THE EARTH DREAMS

BLACK CANADIAN SPECULATIVE STORIES

EDITED BY **TERESE MASON PIERRE**

SPIDERLINE

Copyright © 2025 Terese Mason Pierre
Copyright to each individual piece in this collection is held by the author of that piece.

Published in Canada in 2025 and the USA in 2025 by House of Anansi Press Inc.
houseofanansi.com

All rights reserved. No part of this publication may be reproduced or transmitted in any form or by any means, electronic or mechanical, including photocopying, recording, or any information storage and retrieval system, without permission in writing from the publisher.

House of Anansi Press is committed to protecting our natural environment. This book is made of material from well-managed FSC®-certified forests, recycled materials, and other controlled sources.

House of Anansi Press is a Global Certified Accessible™ (GCA by Benetech) publisher. The ebook version of this book meets stringent accessibility standards and is available to readers with print disabilities.

29 28 27 26 25   1 2 3 4 5

Library and Archives Canada Cataloguing in Publication

Title: As the Earth dreams : Black Canadian speculative stories / edited by Terese Mason Pierre.
Names: Pierre, Terese Mason, editor.
Identifiers: Canadiana (print) 20250227460 | Canadiana (ebook) 20250227479 | ISBN 9781487012663 (softcover) | ISBN 9781487012670 (EPUB)
Subjects: CSH: Speculative fiction, Canadian (English) | CSH: Short stories, Canadian (English) | CSH: Canadian literature (English)—Black Canadian authors. | CSH: Canadian fiction (English)—21st century. | LCSH: Speculative fiction, Canadian. | LCSH: Short stories, Canadian. | LCSH: Canadian fiction—Black authors. | LCSH: Canadian fiction—21st century. | LCGFT: Short stories.
Classification: LCC PS8323.S59 A83 2025 | DDC C813/.087608896071—dc23

Cover design: Greg Tabor
Cover image: © Onyxprj/Dreamstime.com
Interior design and typesetting: Lucia Kim

Lines from "You Don't Know" by Yejide Kilanko (2021) in "The Hole in the Middle of the World" used with permission.

House of Anansi Press is grateful for the privilege to work on and create from the Traditional Territory of many Nations, including the Anishinabeg, the Wendat, and the Haudenosaunee, as well as the Treaty Lands of the Mississaugas of the Credit.

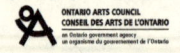

We acknowledge for their financial support of our publishing program the Canada Council for the Arts, the Ontario Arts Council, and the Government of Canada.

Printed and bound in Canada

CONTENTS

INTRODUCTION
Terese Mason Pierre · ix

RAVENOUS, CALLED IFFY
Chimedum Ohaegbu · 1

THE HOLE IN THE MIDDLE OF THE WORLD
Chinelo Onwualu · 19

A FAIR ASSESSMENT
Terese Mason Pierre · 39

PEAK DAY
Suyi Davies Okungbowa · 57

HALLELUJAH HERE AND ELSEWHERE
francesca ekwuyasi · 69

PLAYING DEAD
Trynne Delaney · 93

MOTHER, FATHER, BABY
Lue Palmer · 107

DEH AH MARKET
   Whitney French · 115
PAROXYSM
   Zalika Reid-Benta · 143
JUST SAY GARUKA
   Aline-Mwezi Niyonsenga · 157

ABOUT THE CONTRIBUTORS · 173

INTRODUCTION

Terese Mason Pierre

FOR THOSE WHO AREN'T in the know yet, Canadian speculative literature is only growing, becoming richer and more diverse each year. I have been in speculative literature spaces since my early adulthood, primarily through magazine editing and my work as a poet. As I move further into these communities, especially in Canada, I have been eager to discover and make room for marginalized writers—in particular, Black writers and writers of colour. Black writers have a long and unique relationship to speculative literature, even beyond Afrofuturism.

Speculative writing is an umbrella term that includes fantasy, science fiction, slipstream, horror, apocalyptic, alternate history, and other unreal and imagined writing. When it comes to literature by marginalized writers, we can ask: Who defines *speculative*? What narratives and writings are considered mythology? What is considered realism? Which people—and which legacies and institutions of power—get to discriminate between the real world and the unreal?

Nowadays, how can we unpack the speculative within the historical and political project of Canadian literature? We can ask: How can we revere and honour the stories and imaginations—heard and unheard, lost and unearthed—of the oppressed and the marginalized? What does it mean for Black people to tell stories with this history, and write ourselves into the future? How does the label of speculative shape Black writing? It is in this speculating where we find the deepest well of imagination, declaration, and augury.

This anthology seeks to reveal and uplift the spectacular writing by Black writers in Canada. I wanted to showcase the immense talent within our borders, from voices established and emerging. I looked for writers across the country, whose relationships to Canada and to the speculative genre were as diverse as their stories. The title *As the Earth Dreams* centres the idea of limitless imagination, particularly for Black writers in speculative literature. What worlds and futures can we experiment with and speculate on? What would happen if we held space for joy, friendship, and desire? What do our fears reveal about what we yearn for, or regret most? All within the same anthology. Through working with these marvellous writers, and reading their work, *As the Earth Dreams* transformed into a work that is hopeful, eclectic, and honest.

The stories in this anthology explore living and dead

relationships, ancestry and inheritance, love and desire, natural and urban landscapes, labour and leisure, secrets and truths. They step into future and memory, speculate on and through societies foreign and familiar, but never stray from deeply human relationships, with self and others. *Haunting* is an apt descriptor for many of the stories, while some also celebrate connection, healing, and life.

In this anthology, a masseuse attends her mother's fourth funeral, a prelude to her latest resurrection, only to encounter family she's never met. A postdoc instructor navigates an almost-life in an Elsewhere realm of safety and comfort. A pair of cousins bend time and space to connect with worlds and relatives past. After societal collapse, an immigrant leaves her precarious station, and her memories, behind. A woman isolating from a new virus starts hallucinating. A corporate worker learns about the true nature of their workplace. A young nanny accepts a job with a peculiar employer in search of immortality. A medium is tasked with summoning a spirit that hits too close to home. A woman confined by shadows and sounds confronts, and makes peace with, a death. And two teenagers test a friendship over magic carpet flying practice.

As the Earth Dreams furthers conversations of growth, futurity, and joy that are necessary in Canadian literature spaces. These stories ask: How can we hold on to memories we've lost? How can we remain true to ourselves under capitalism and collapse? How can the worlds around us facilitate our growth? What pain and shame do we need to let go of, and what do we keep? What promises can we make to each other, and how can we connect to our past? How can we dream of something new, and better?

I hope that readers enjoy these stories as much as I have, and venture into their own speculation, choosing work and worlds that reframe reality, reflect the internal, and hold space for dreaming.

RAVENOUS, CALLED IFFY

Chimedum Ohaegbu

MY NAME IS RAVENOUS, like the city, but I much prefer Ifeoma. My mother named me what she named me because Ravenous is where she's from and ravenous is what she is. Was. She said, often, that she had nothing else of herself to give me. Patently untrue, this statement. She gave me: the slope of her chin and the flair of her nostrils, the thickness of her hair and waist, and her astigmatism, also, to say nothing of her short stature and fondness for pickled, vinegary flavours. When I smile, I'm all resemblance. She could have named me after herself.

The name I got was unsuitable, unnecessary—overkill, even. Imagine: Ravenous, when I was disallowed from fasting for being too skilled at it and making my peers jealous during Hungry Masses; Ravenous, when it should have been obvious from the moment of my birth that I was too uncertain and boring to ever call to mind something as complex as a town, let alone a city. (I was more of an over-large suburb at best.)

The most interesting thing about me, aside from my name, is the fact that my current pair of glasses are octagonal. After my mother's third death, I waited. Usually resurrection was quick; she should have been back within days, at most a month. I waited while I worked the muscles of the aching at the massage clinic; I waited while testing my newest cocktails on Hen and soliciting her opinions; I waited while I waited for the bus to take me to bartending classes, the library, the graveyard where my mother had been buried. One year passed in waiting, and then it became clear to me—despite Hen's gentle, sweet-hearted optimism on my behalf—that my mother's lives had run their course and she didn't have another resurrection in her.

So the new glasses were me trying to be fashionable. Hen suggested I do this in an attempt to "brighten up my life." If it's working, I can't tell, but I don't have the money yet to replace the frames, so octagonal I will be. Fake-fashionable is better than ravenous and better than Ravenous. Please, I tell everyone—patients at the massage clinic, my classmates' daughters, telemarketers, Hen when I first knew her—please, call me Ifeoma. It means "good thing"; and I know I could be good.

•

THE INVITATION COMES IN the mail and it startles me.

I'm just back from Hen's place, where I spent an unfruitful morning trying to forgive her over tea and rusk and some softer pastries left over from her man's office party. I've gone sour in the attempt, and so, sighting the mail carrier sets my shoulders to sagging even lower.

Still, it isn't her fault that Hen's gotten herself pregnant and will soon be married; it isn't the mail carrier's fault that Hen had taken it into her head to ask me to be the baby's godmother. I can't blame the mail carrier for the warmth of Hen's hand on mine, the pang of pre-emptive nostalgia this gave me. The flowers and cake and song and dance, the kiss and vows between Hen and her man to come, none of these can reasonably be said to be the mail carrier's fault; and it's always nice to have someone to talk to. I'll soon be in need of friends anyway.

Straightening my shoulders, I tap the mail carrier on hers and say, "Good morning!"

The woman jumps—people always react to me as if I've snuck up on them; I've taken to wearing louder shoes, but these don't work on grass—but smiles once her gaze leaves my face. She is the age my mother had been when she died the second time.

The mail carrier says, "Good morning. Caught you just in time, it seems."

"Yes."

I don't know what to say then and only smile, at a loss. The deliverer rallies: "Ravenous A———?"

"Ifeoma."

"So this isn't for you?"

"Oh—no, I'm sorry. It is," I say, annoyed with myself. "Thank you."

"There's also mail for Jessaline and Treasure."

"My roommates. I can take those in too, thank you." I hesitate, then ask, "Would you like a strawberry strudel?"

We trade. I get the invitation, fundraising queries for Jess, and a magazine subscription for Treasure, while the deliverer makes off with the leftovers that Hen, pity-struck and showing, pushed onto me as I fled her home. A crust of sugar still nasties my teeth. I enter the apartment licking them smooth, jerking the serrated edge of my house key through the top of the envelope to open it. Then I stop walking, stop breathing, the better to concentrate on what I'm reading. This is what I learn from the invitation:

My mother has died again, apparently for the fourth time—though I'd only known of her first three deaths;

The funeral will be held in Ravenous, my namesake;

My half-siblings—I have siblings?—will be in attendance.

To the door I turn first, thinking *help*, thinking *Hen!* But then I stop short again. I don't want Hen reading my expressions or movements in the wake of this news and her own. My voice, at least, won't betray me. So I lift the phone and press it to my ear, comforted by the cool, oily plastic.

Except I don't remember Hen's number. Usually I just go to her house.

Against my better angels, I glance back at the invitation. I learn more: a carriage will be sent for me. It will arrive tomorrow and ferry me to Ravenous in style, a trip of some hours.

Darkness drops slowly. My bedroom beckons and I slip in just as my roommates are entering the front door. Shutting mine, I sigh. A funeral tomorrow, for a fourth death.

My mother's second death—I wasn't born yet when she'd endured and beaten her first—had nothing to do with me or my wickedness or politeness or lack of ravenousness or my poor parodies of goodness. No matter what the papers have insinuated in the time since. No—no. It went like this: she hid, she was heard, she was hurt, then she was hidden. The funeral was closed casket. The manhunt for her killer went on for one million years, then they found him, then they put him to the chair and let him thrash to death by lightning. Why was she killed? No one could tell me. I went to her funeral and I went to his frying and I wept each time, though once was out of joy and the other grief. I haven't cried since. Not even when Jess's cat Carrot, who was really more my cat, died; not even when the bus didn't come and the snow piled high and I trudged home empty-hearted and lonesome; not this morning, learning about Hen.

Not even now, definitely not now, hearing the merriment of those I live with outside, holding in my shaking hands an envelope, a letter, an invitation, to my mother's fourth funeral, with dates that indicate that five years have elapsed between her rebirth and this new death, a time in which I have seen her not *once*, not at all, even though I waited, I didn't move away from where she left me, and she could have found me easily, easily, if she'd wanted, because I've been right here. I've always been right here.

•

SOME CITIES BEGIN IN fits and spurts. A couple houses here, then the silence of the road again. Then a shantytown or landfill, which only briefly interrupt the ongoing countryside. Then at last a welcome sign and gas stations for incoming or outgoing travellers, prologuing the main event, which, at last, rises to meet you.

Other cities are ruder, exist abruptly. In the span of a blink you can move between farmland and outrageous urbanity—strip malls and residences, traffic jams popping up quick as pimples—the line demarcating them almost akin to natural phenomena in its undeniability.

The incidence of the city of Ravenous occurs as a gradient. Translucence is how it begins: I look outside and see shimmers, but can only catch them in the corner of my eye. When I look down my body is similarly see-through. Does the city think I'm joining its citizenry? Or does it call to something in my blood, which is my mother's blood, and claim it? I realize that I can't think of what you'd call someone from Ravenous; historically I've only ever called such people "Mother," which cannot be the correct demonym for everyone else. Ravenites? Ravening? The other ghosts and I shimmer. So does the sound of the horses' hoofbeats, the decibels thinner than they were when we were in my hometown.

I bounce a bit in my seat as we go over potholes and heat-expanded, cracked concrete. Ravenous and its people deepen with every minute of progress the carriage makes, until the insubstantiality resolves into outlines, then the outlines into etchings, then the etchings into buildings, plants, animals, and people whose solidity, at last, would resist me if I were to try to put a hand through them and vice-versa.

"What was that?" I call to the driver. His name is Daniel, and he's from here.

"What was what?"

"We were …" I wave my hand in front of my face, hiding it then revealing it again. "An hour ago, on the outskirts, I couldn't do that. I wasn't opaque."

"Well, you're grieving," he reminds me, and speeds the horse.

I don't cry but I quiet down. We ride into Ravenous city centre early in the evening. I'm realizing that I've been picturing a city some twenty years out of date, based on the stories of my mother, who hasn't been back since she left—since her father bade her go. In my mind, Ravenous is sunbaked and sedate, lively and dangerous. People dress better back home, my mother said. People carry themselves differently, because everyone talks to everyone, and if you're looking ragged at the market it's because you've always secretly held a ragged heart, were sired from ragdoll folk, and have a destiny of raggedness awaiting you and any venture you undertake. In Ravenous, I gathered, people are willing to embarrass one another, the daughters are prettier, the rivalries more humanely dealt with, and the tinned sardines have actual flavour. From the stories of my mother I imagined Ravenous as a hungering place, one that demands your best, then turns that best to compete against others', and gives its best in return.

But I find that as I step down from the bus, it's thirst that is far more pressing than hunger. The air here is drier than in my humid, seaside hometown. I get a drink of mango juice, thinking about how my mother used to ride the buses here by jumping and latching onto the frames of moving vehicles, how I did so as a child too in my own hometown, and always felt closer to her in so doing. One passes me by, buffeting me with a wind smelling of clay and sweat-spattered cloth, the rosy perfume of one of its hanging-on passengers. By the time I consider hopping on and mimicking my mother's youth and my own, the bus has gone on its sagging way.

There's mango pulp on my mouth. I meet the first half of my half-siblings holding a sign that says *IFFY* and calling out the same, which would be kind of him if it didn't indicate that my mother had spoken of me to him, instead of coming back to me and telling tale of him.

Still, I go over. He will take me to her. Apparently she can still resurrect, so I'll ask her about all this when she's up.

•

IT'S A PARTY, NOT a funeral, and everyone here is unknown to me. The carriage driver was a stranger and so are the priests. My half-siblings—I've two, Adanna and Peter, the latter meeting me at the station—are strange, and look at me strangely. Jealousy might be the motive. Neither of them so closely resemble my mother as I do. Adanna, for her part, is tall and slim, with light skin hailing from her father's side of the family. Peter does have our mother's chin, but he's wiry, hairy, and silly—maybe from his own father. When he picked me up at the station he said, "It's good to see you again."

I'd wanted the first word, to weaponize my ignorance of him as evidence of his unimportance rather than of my distance, to say, *I've never heard of you. She never mentioned a son. But it's good to meet you.*

But I was thrown off by his warmth and his words, his strange words. "Again?"

"We met when you were a baby," he explained. "I'd have been three or four."

"Oh." I smiled, off-put. "I wish I could say the same."

He'd taken me not to a funeral, as I'd expected, but to a house full of people who said they loved my mother and were excited for her to come back. Whoever had sent my invitation had had the times confused, it seemed, and I made it for the funeral *reception* rather than the starting event.

I drink deeply of the fruit punch they've set out. It could use a twist of lime, a salt-rimmed cup. Even though Peter and Adanna are also half-siblings, they actually know one another; I watch them talk across the room. In Ravenous people all walk and sit upright. Nobody slouches that I can see. Maybe that's why my mother left? But then why be buried here? Why did she spend the last five years here and not tell me, or take me with her? My siblings might be talking about some fond memory they have of our mother from the recent past, when I thought her to be in the ground still. I should have dug her up, I should've checked. Hen wasn't yet pregnant nor betrothed; she would've helped me. I can almost see the grave dirt on her face now, and the thought warms me.

"Thanks, Iffy," says Adanna with surprise. I'm surprised also; I didn't realize I'd brought myself over, hadn't noticed the clench of my teeth. There are two cups of punch sweating in my hands, held out to Adanna and Peter. They take the cups and Peter says, "Cheers, to Mum!"

We cheers. I don't have a drink, so I simply raise a fist. While they sip I say, "I haven't seen you two at the other funerals. What's so special about this one?"

They wipe their mouths in an identical action. I can't tell if it's an heirloom I've missed out on or learned behaviour from getting to be siblings, but I find fault either way, and press them: "Who sent out the invitations for this?

There was some kind of error or mismanagement with the planning of this, I think—I should've been here earlier."

Peter says, "Mum did."

I have to ignore that so I return to my original question, reword it. "Why weren't either of you at the other funerals?"

Adanna smiles angrily. "I was told I wasn't needed."

"I wasn't told at all," Peter says, one-upping her. Adanna's smile tightens, and she excuses herself to speak to one of the priests. Now it's just my brother and I. I'm having more trouble finding my mother in his face now. He says, "Tell me, Iffy, how were those funerals? Did Mum like them?"

"She had a good time, yes." It's grating that he calls her *Mum* and not *Mother*. I'm not going to let Peter be the most wronged party here. "I'm sorry to hear you weren't told. She bounced back quickly, anyway."

Before she died the second time, my mother disagreed with my assessment about the inappropriateness of my name, and also with my propensity for anything resembling goodness. Her evidence is one of my stranger memories. One honey-sunshine day my mother was detangling my hair, adding coconut oil to make it shine. She was humming a song to herself that I knew only as "Lullaby," though was it really a lullaby if she sang it to me at all hours?

Unless she wanted me always to be asleep, which considering my wickedness makes sense.

In any case she was humming "Lullaby" until she said,

"Hold on just a moment while I get more coconut oil; your hair is growing longer and you need much more of it now." I beamed up at her, though not for the reason she believed: as soon as she left I used the excess oil in my hair to draw upon the mirror. I gazed at myself through the smear of my words and rather liked the look of them upon my face, as if I were a letter to the world.

My mother came back and saw the words and gasped and demanded of me, then, and then later, and still later, where I'd learned such language—then later, when her confusion and disgust mellowed into pure bewilderment, when I'd learned to write.

The worst of it is that I don't remember what I wrote. I was very young at the time—apparently, though, this was some time after I'd "met" Peter—and didn't write again until I was taught how to do it right, to do it well, to do it good. Even when I asked her later, my mother never ever told me the words I'd smeared onto our mirror.

Now I tell Peter, "I didn't even know she was back until I got the letter saying she was gone again."

Peter grimaces, licks at the dregs of punch in his cup. "She was gone a long time, yes. But that's just because she had some trouble regenerating—she'd been away from Ravenous"—he glances at me; did I respond to that?—"for too long."

"Everyone here does that?"

"Resurrects?" Peter shakes his head. "No. It's more like everyone who *can* do that is from here."

"Can you?"

"Kill me and find out," he says. At my stare he chuckles: strange he is, as I've said, and silly. "I'm joking. Adanna wouldn't like it if I upstaged Mum at her own reception and awakening."

"Wait—she's to be back *tonight*?"

"That's what she told me."

I haven't even accomplished anything in the time she's been gone except mourning her and losing Hen. I thought I'd be abandoned for longer, forever, but it barely exceeded the time since I learned I *was* abandoned. I tell Peter I'm going to get some fresh air, and he nods as though this is what I was expected to say.

•

IN THE CLINIC I am well-liked by my patients, tolerated by my coworkers. As for the work itself ... six years in and yet, the warmth of human skin still sometimes startled me so badly that I couldn't tell the heat of fever from that of life. Rare for this to shake me, but when rarity ran out my fingertips lay featherlight and static on the patient's back as I gathered myself.

Grounding exercises helped. Things I could see: my hands, hesitant; the nape of the client's neck lying in wait; the diffuser sighing white steam; white, too, were the blankets. Smells—the diffuser's citrus-brightened cinnamon; deodorant; and depending on the brand and strength of the deodorant, the patient's mild-to-moderate-to-milky body odour. The flavours: bile on the rise, scorpion-bitter and just as quick; the morning's mint gum, chewed now past irrelevance and all the way into tautology, making my mouth taste only of my mouth; and my mouth. Two things to hear: inhale, exhale. And I knew what I touched.

When I was being lazy, a cruder attitude adjustment was in order instead. Six years in, and despite that, sometimes the heat multiplying beneath my palms would not seem innocent until I asked myself, *Ifeoma, is their back warm, or are your hands just cold?*

All a matter of perspective. According to this mindset, I'd not once encountered a sick person, and never would.

Outside in the garden I breathe in magnolia and work my fingers over my forearm, trying to do unto myself what I do unto others for money. My arms are tight, my jaw is clenched, and I'm drying up out here. It isn't clear to me why my mother wanted me here for her death but not the last few years of her life. I don't know what I did wrong, which means I can't avoid doing it again and once more earning my loneliness.

My poor forearm! The harder I rub, the more unsure I get about why my patients feel my touch is helpful. I irritate myself. I wish I liked cigarettes, so I could have a little light. I press my thumb into my abductor and do no good. I wonder if the patients lie, if everyone is lying to me. Then again, when Hen told me the truth, I had to and failed to find it in myself to forgive her for it. So maybe dishonesty is the best way I can be treated.

Adanna comes out. *She* has a cigarette. My mother's favourite brand, Ordain, too. When she sees me she nods and I remember that she is my mother's first daughter and has the cigarette-smell to prove it.

I swallow. There's hardly any saliva in my mouth and my throat audibly clicks with the effort. "Do you live here?"

"In Ravenous? No. I'm from B——," she says, another seaside city.

"Was Mother in your life the last few years?"

"She wrote me letters."

I cease my efforts upon my forearm. "Oh."

"Nothing hugely detailed, Iffy," Adanna says. She takes a quick drag of her cigarette and blows smoke, away from me at least. "Status updates. Progress reports."

"Was she working on something?"

Adanna frowns at me. "Wasn't she always?"

"Not during my childhood."

"Then yours was very different than mine."

With some coaxing I manage to get her to talk about her life. In B—— she worked as a necromancer; she couldn't be sure if *she* had the resurrection gene without going through the worst, obviously, but was interested in seeing other people raised up in the meantime. Part of why she wasn't necessary at our mother's other funerals is that necromantic energies sometimes interfere with organic self-resurrection.

"Then why are you at this one?"

"Why are you?"

I flinch. "What do you mean?" Although I too have wondered this. I'm not sure what my presence means anymore.

Instead of answering, Adanna tilts her head to listen to a cheer go up from inside. I'm suddenly frightened that my mother, our mother, has awoken, or that Adanna has, as warned, somehow ruined Mother's return just by being here.

It can't be either because the cheer dies down back to regular chatter soon enough. Someone must have done a party trick. Adanna says, "If a resurrection takes place in Ravenous then no necromantic presence can make it go wrong, don't worry." She adds without malice, "You really do look a lot like her."

"You're the eldest daughter." I don't know why I'm comforting her. Nor do I know why I think this should comfort her. "At least she wrote to you."

Adanna smiles, not at me. I think I've had my fill of this, and make as if to go back inside, expecting Adanna to come along. When I take a glance back, she's still finishing her cigarette, a light in the darkness surrounded by smoke.

•

A QUARTER HOUR PASSES, during which I feast upon chin chin and scowl away conversation. Then, near to midnight, Peter says it's time and begins gathering people up out of the corners and crooks of the house, chasing them from the garden to the main room. Adanna walks in with a new cigarette in hand. The priests clear a space in the middle of the floor and dance a coffin over to the circle drawn upon the tiles.

They open the coffin. My mother, she looks older but well. It occurs to me I have no idea how she died, just as I don't know how she's been living lately.

The priests begin singing an anti-lullaby, more to set the mood than anything else—my mother's return doesn't quite require them, it's more of a nice touch. Peter nods his head along to the music. Adanna rolls her shoulders. I'm reciting things to myself, reminders of what I can do to make it more in my mother's interests for her to leave Ravenous once she's up and come back and live with me again.

Historically my mother has liked butterflies, shortbread, matinees, Ordain cigarettes, Scott Joplin piano tunes. I'll raise caterpillars into monarchs, I'll buy out the supermarkets' supply of sugar and butter and bake them together, I'll reserve every theatre for noontime, I'll get into smoking, I'll give up on playing muscle to tickle the ivory. I can be Ravenous, if she misses it so damn badly. I won't make her apologize; my forgiveness is reserved for Hen anyway.

I watch the face of my mother, and I wait for it to change. If it's between one Ravenous and another, I have to make it so I'm the victorious one. I watch her, making the face I want her to make, hoping she copies me when she opens her eyes like a baby bird might, waiting for her to sight me and smile and ask, *What could I love, if not you? Who could I love, if not this?*

THE HOLE IN THE MIDDLE OF THE WORLD
Chinelo Onwualu

You don't know what it is that you are looking for. But you can feel its absence when your fingers reach out and come up short. When the knot in the middle of your chest tightens and causes splinters from your frame. How does one miss so badly what one does not know?
—Yejide Kilanko, "You Don't Know" (2021)

"WHEN DID YOU GIVE BIRTH?"

I'm lying on the cracked plastic examination table, my legs hitched up in stirrups, as the white woman who is today's obstetric-gynecologist at the Memory Store parts the lips of my labia with one finger of her blue-gloved hand. She touches my body with the studied professionalism of someone who's been trained to do something deeply unpleasant. It reminds me of some of my johns.

I am willing myself to remain still under her hands, so it takes a moment to register her words.

"I don't have any kids," I say.

Her face scrunches into something approximating sympathy. But she's no actress; I can tell she doesn't care.

"I'm sorry for your loss," she says automatically and reaches for the speculum.

"No," I say, rising on my elbows to look directly at the woman bent over between my legs. "You don't understand, I've *never* had children. I've never given birth."

Her expression hardens, a look I can tell she's more comfortable with. "You don't have to talk about it if you don't want to, but you shouldn't lie to your doctors."

"Why would I lie about this?"

"I don't know, people lie about all kinds of things," she says primly as she lubes up the tool. We both hear the missing *like you* in that phrase.

"Honey, I'm a hooker not your priest," I sass. "I don't lie unless I'm being paid."

She looks me in the eye as she jams the cold metal into my vagina and, with no warning, wrenches it open. I grit my teeth and bite back a cry.

"Sorry," she says with a cold smile. I hold her gaze until she drops hers.

The monthly health examination over, I walk slowly back to my quarters in the refugee zone. The pain between my legs has lessened to a dull throbbing. I want to rage at this latest humiliation, but my anger will not kindle. It's just one of the many routine degradations I'm expected to gratefully endure for the institutional generosity of my presence in the land of my betters. But if I'm never allowed to forget who I am, then neither should they.

This area used to be rock quarries; it is devoid of the rich greenery that characterizes the rest of the city. Here, the air tastes like grit and dust. My "quarters" are the top of an undersized bunk bed in a two-room microunit, one of hundreds crammed into the five prefab buildings set aside for single and childless refugees. Of my six other roommates, only one is home today, a broad-bodied woman with the nut-brown colouring of one of the drowned Pacific Islands. Though we've lived in the same space for nearly a year, she and I have yet to exchange a word. I don't even know her name. She is sleeping off her long night shift at the elder care facility and will likely still be in bed when I leave for my official work detail at the city's mail sorting hub in an hour or two. I fetch my bucket and bathing kit from my locker at the foot of the bed and head to the communal bathroom at the end of the hall.

The bathroom is blessedly empty at this time of the day—just after the workers of the morning shifts have left and long after the night shifts have returned. Today's waterflow is uncertain but running. There's even hot water, though it peters out after a few minutes. I bathe vigorously, trying to get the feel of the Memory Store's clinic off my skin.

This is not the first time I've been asked about my birth status. The rich white folk of this country can't seem to birth babies on their own anymore, so it looks like they've kicked up their search for surrogates among us refugees and immigrants. There's really nothing they won't buy, is there? These days though, the question snags at something in me. A hole, a vast abyssal emptiness at the core of my being. I want to cry, but I don't know why. I just can't shake the feeling that I've forgotten something deeply important.

I scoop water out of the bucket with a small plastic bowl and pour it over my body. As I scrub, I run my hands critically over myself. Does the flop of my lower belly indicate a pregnancy? Are my sagging breasts because of breastfeeding? I close my eyes and crook my arms, imagining that I am cradling a baby. The act feels oddly familiar. I open my eyes again and take in the cracked grey tile of the shower stall. I try to picture a child in this bleak space and there my imagination runs aground. This is no place for that kind of innocence.

A white envelope is waiting for me on my bed when I return from the bathroom. It has an official government seal at one corner. My roommate is still sleeping. Whoever dropped the letter off hadn't woken her. My name is misspelled, as usual, but my status number is correct, which is all that matters. Inside the envelope is a cheque for the largest amount of money I've ever seen. It's backdated to a year ago, which tells me it's been processing through the system for a while, and has been issued for "services rendered."

I cross-check the National Bank stamp at the bottom. I hold the slim sheet of mushroom paper up to the dim lightbulb in the ceiling to illuminate the hidden hologram on the back of the check.

Yep, it's legit.

I dress quickly and gather my things—including my little good luck pebble, the odd black pyramid I take everywhere with me. I don't bother returning my bucket to the locker. I head out the door and I don't look back.

• •

THEY TELL ME THE owner of this apartment is actually thirteen years old. His parents got it for him so he'd have his own place when he goes to college. They rent it to the government as a halfway home for refugee families so it can earn him income in the meantime. I can't begin to imagine that kind of wealth. I've never owned more than I could fit into a suitcase.

It's a compact one-bedroom with stark cream walls and angular, modern furnishings in white fabrics and blond wood. I can't seem to get warm here, no matter how high I turn up the heat.

The little girl with me seems just as uncomfortable in the space as I am. Her name is Nomi. She's got to be about seven or eight years old—no more than ten, though she often seems much younger. I don't remember when she first showed up. She must have been assigned to my care, but I've got no paperwork to prove it. She's a war orphan, I suspect. She has that shell-shocked look kids get when they've seen too much, experienced too much. She barely speaks, but she's always nearby, like she's afraid I'll disappear if she takes her eyes off me. She insists on sleeping in the same bed as me and calls me "Momma." I've stopped correcting her. If it makes her feel safer, I'll allow it. There *is* a familiarity to her I can't explain. When I hold her, she feels right in my arms. Like she belongs there.

She's sharper than a blade, this kid. With a memory like a vault—always knows where the keys are, if the stove's still on, if we locked the door when we left the house. Me, I don't even remember moving into this place.

It's not like I have amnesia or anything, it's just that the further in time I think back to, the clearer my memories are. I can remember what life was like in the States before the insurrection, when girls could go to school and Black people could drive and own things. I remember all those years in the Natchez labour camps—the relentless claustrophobic heat of the slaughterhouses, the whippings, the screams in the middle of the night. But I can't remember exactly how I escaped, or how I got to this cold, featureless apartment. Whenever I try, it's like trying to catch catfish in a muddy pool with my bare hands. The memories keep slipping just out of my grasp.

I care for the kid as best I can, make sure she's clean, fed, and well-rested. I get her to school every day, and I pick her up. I soothe her when she's upset, I nurse her when she's sick. Every night, I tell her stories. Stories from my own childhood about Brer Fox and Brer Rabbit, and Tortoise, and Anansi the Spider. I even crib the stories I learned from a book of European fairy tales I stole from the library when I was her age—though I put a kinder spin on them than the originals. White folk are a bloodthirsty bunch, even in the stories they tell their children. I take her with me on my safer jobs, like at the mail centre. And at the end of each week, when I get back from the Memory Store, I make sure to take her out for a treat. I mean, we're both alone in this big country; we've got to look out for each other.

One day, I take her to the beach. I mean, it's really a lakeshore, nothing like the real beaches I grew up with. There's no sea salt smell in the air, no rhythmic crashing of the surf. The sand is smooth, with a greyish-white tinge to it. It feels like a poor digital copy, like someone's idea of a beach that's not quite right. The kid loves it, though. She laughs that bright, infectious laugh of hers and runs up and down the shore like a kitten with the 3:00 a.m. zoomies.

I'm looking off at the water, and it reminds me of something. Something I can't quite remember …

Starla and me on the deck of Poppa's speedboat, holding tight to our seats as it skips across the surface of a choppy sea. Whenever we hit a wave, the whole boat is lifted clear out of the water. When it crashes down, the surf sprays across my face—

"Momma?"

I blink and look at the little girl in front of me. She's offering me a rock; the kid loves collecting rocks. This one is shaped like a rough pyramid, smooth and black with a pearlescent sheen. I take it from her.

"It's to help you remember me," she says in a hollow voice. She looks like a child who has had one too many promises broken. "Do you like it?"

"I love it. Thank you, sugarcube."

• • •

THE TWENTY-FOUR-HOUR DINER IS tucked in the middle of the strip of businesses that line the roadway to our building. There are two grocery stores, a pharmacy, a repair café that fixes everything from broken vacuums to worn-out shoes, a couple of restaurants, a small clothier where you can get a decent outfit for your work detail, and a combo barber-hair salon. Even though these are the only government-licenced shops within walking distance of the newly created refugee zone, an area that houses nearly one thousand migrants and refugees, they are almost always empty. Most of us can't afford these retailers and their sanctioned prices. The few of us who can buy outside rations only use them to barter for what we really need on the inside.

That's right, the few of *us*. My paperwork finally came through. After five and a half years of status limbo, we can now get our groceries from government commissaries instead of our neighbours. I can get my Nomi into a certified daycare instead of relying on the Somali aunties on our floor; at six she's overdue to start school anyway. And I can stop turning tricks for third-rate johns and get a job I can take my kid to.

Ever since that night in Natchez when me—seventeen and pregnant—and five others stuffed ourselves into the back of a refrigerated truck and headed north to escape, I've been holding my breath. It finally feels like I can breathe again.

Nomi and I pass this diner every morning when we head downtown. Her to the crèche where she'll spend her day learning the letters and manners of our new home, me to the employment centre where I'll grab whatever job I can find until my official work detail is assigned. We've never had enough money to go inside before, but today is different.

Today, I sold my first cognitive asset to the Memory Store.

Of course, I don't know what the asset was—that's kind of the point of selling a memory. I don't feel any different, so it probably wasn't anything important anyway. And the money? Well, the money is very, very good.

Normally, my kid will run ahead, ignoring my calls to return until I chase her down and scoop her up. But ever since we left the Cognitive Diagnosis and Recovery Clinic—what we newcomers have taken to calling "the Memory Store"—she's been quiet, holding my hand tight as if afraid I'll disappear.

"Hey sugarcube, what do you say we go in for a treat?"

"A treat?"

"Yeah, like ice cream." Nomi's eyes light up at the term. She'd discovered the concept in a book we read a few months ago and she's been pestering me for some ever since.

"Ice cream!" she declares happily as we enter the store.

Walking into the diner feels like entering a dream. There's a short counter with a clear glass display in front where fake replicas of cakes and sandwiches sit under soft yellow lights. Beyond it, clusters of round tables surrounded by high stools dot the store. A wide screen above us shows the full menu and its prices. I remember places like this from when I was a kid in New Orleans—before the insurrection and the Christian Nationalists. Before an accusation of being "woke" could set your whole family up for re-education.

I lift Nomi onto one of the two seats at the counter and take up the other one. A bored-looking white man in his forties or fifties silently watches as I place our order on the data pad. He didn't bother to greet us when we came in and doesn't speak as he sloppily preps the two servings of chocolate—the real stuff, too, not the artificially flavoured kind you get these days—ice cream. When he's done, he shoves them in front of us. I note that he's used lidded takeout bowls even though I'd ordered them for eating in. He pretends not to hear when I ask for a second spoon, and I have to use my "ethnic voice" to get his attention. I side-eye him as he clatters the plastic spoon on the counter before disappearing to the back. I'm glad to be free of his obvious resentment.

"Not my fault you fucked up your life so bad that this

is your work detail," I yell loud enough for him to hear. "You're a citizen, you're white, you're male—you won the fucking lottery! Make better choices next time!"

I kiss my teeth as I pick up the two bowls, and I hear Nomi next to me doing the same. When did she learn to do that? I turn to her, and she beams at me with that mischievous gap-toothed grin of hers. Laughing, I help her down from the stool and we head out of the store.

Outside, we sit side-by-side on a nearby bench, letting the late summer sun warm our faces. Beyond us, past the strip of green verge, across the wide black tarmac of the road, are the hulking shapes of construction cranes and earth movers erecting more prefab units like our building. As the world beyond this country's borders falls further and further apart, there'll be more refugees and immigrants. Best to be prepared.

As I taste the first spoonful of cold sweetness, I'm transported to a memory I thought I'd buried decades ago …

My mom and I, sitting on a park bench in the French Quarter. The smell of jasmine from nearby bushes filling the air. I'm in my Sunday whites, my shiny black court shoes glinting in the late afternoon light. She's in her good hat and dress, fanning herself with a church bulletin as she gossips with the other aunties after service. The wind rustles the trees, and the taste of chocolate is rich on my tongue … And … And—

"Momma!" I snap out of my reverie.

Nomi is standing in front of me, her eyes wide in alarm. In one hand, she's clutching her spoon like a weapon, ice cream dripping forgotten down her wrist. With the other, she has grabbed my sleeve.

"Momma! Where were you?" Her voice is on the edge of panic. She asked me the same question at the clinic right after I came out of the procedure.

I blink at her and struggle to remember what I was just thinking about. But the memory has evaporated like a drop of water on a hot skillet. Gone before I can catch its edges.

"I'm right here, sugarcube," I say. "Always."

••••

GOLD EVENING LIGHT HITS Nomi's face just so, turning her skin the colour of fresh-baked bread and highlighting a smattering of white crumbs at the side of her mouth. I brush them away with my thumb, grazing my knuckles across her soft cheek as I do. She shifts and snuggles deeper into my arms, nuzzling the side of her face against my chest. I'm folded uncomfortably into one of the low government-issued chairs in the Basic Income Office waiting room and holding her on my lap like precious cargo. At three, she's still small enough to fit comfortably in the crook of my embrace. Her feet, though, splay over either side of me and nearly brush the ground. She's going to be as tall as her mother someday.

We've been waiting for four hours already, naptime has come and gone, and dinnertime is fast approaching. But I can't afford to leave. That'll mean coming back at the ass-crack of dawn tomorrow and joining back at the end of the line because everybody else braved the winter cold and waited through the night. We don't have legal status yet, so we need this voucher if we want this month's groceries to come from a government commissary instead of from bartering with the other residents of our building.

"Letters E to G please come to window four," a computer-generated voice drones through the overhead loudspeakers.

Nomi startles awake as I surge to my feet amid a mad panic of people rushing to be the first to line up at the appropriate window. I want to shout that we all have tags with our numbers on it but I understand that for refugees like us, tags and wait slips are just formalities. In most places in the world, it only matters who gets to the front of the line first. Nomi wraps her long legs around my waist and clutches at my neck. I hunch over my child, hooking one hand under her butt and throwing the other protectively over the back of her head. The tide of people breaks around us. At six foot-two in flats, my body has always been my advantage.

We're not the only family here, and I'm careful to allow those with children younger than mine to cut in front of me. I elbow the lone man who tries to push past me, though. He turns to body check me, but I've taken on bigger and tougher. I give him my full "Do. Not. Fuck. With. Me." glare, and he stands down.

A rough semblance of a line finally forms and we're close enough to the window that I know we'll definitely get a voucher today. Whether that will happen before the office closes is anybody's guess. Nomi is too frightened by the crowd to let me put her down, so I shift my baby to one hip and settle down to wait again. When my arm begins to ache, I shift her to my other arm to get some relief.

About ten minutes in, she begins to fret. "Momma, I'm hungry," she says plaintively and lays a head on my shoulder.

I dig into my satchel for the half of a bagel sandwich that I'd saved from breakfast that morning. I usually grab one from the twenty-four-hour diner at the corner when I'm done working the streets at night. A half sandwich, a hot shower, three or four hours of sleep and I'm ready for the next day.

Nomi gnaws hungrily at the food. I keep our shared water flask ready so she can sip between bites. Once she's eaten, she perks up and begins a running commentary on everything she sees around her.

"What's that?" she asks, pointing at the flatscreen set in a metal pillar by the kiosk.

"An ID reader, it makes sure our identity cards are real."

"That lady is wearing a big hat!"

"That's not a hat, that's a headscarf. Many women from West Africa wear 'em."

"Are you from West Africa?"

"Me? Nah, baby, I'm from Louisiana. But our people were from Nigeria."

"I'm from Nigeria too!"

"That's true. But since you were born here, you're also from here."

"No, I'm not. I'm from Nigeria," she's gearing up to argue in her typical toddler way, so I distract her by pointing to the white woman with the digital clipboard who is walking back and forth along the line.

"What colour's her shirt, sugarcube?"

"Red!" Nomi calls out happily. "And she has black pants on."

Her voice is high and sweet with a slight lisp, as if it's been calibrated by the gods for prime adorableness. No one who hears it can resist a smile. The woman is no exception. And like every white woman who's ever seen a cute black baby, she comes up and leans down over Nomi, exclaiming, "Well, aren't you the cutest little thing!" It's the same tone you'd use on a Pomeranian in a sweater. "And look at your hair! Someone's *certainly* been taking care of you."

I shift Nomi to my other hip, just before the woman's grasping claw can bury itself in my baby's mass of soft curls. The act clearly annoys the woman because she straightens and fixes me with a grim expression, as if registering my existence for the first time.

"Is this your child?" she asks sharply.

I raise an eyebrow at her. "Excuse me?"

"Is this your *biological* child?" she asks impatiently.

"Now, I don't know how that's any of your business."

"I'm with Child Protective Services. I'm an enforcement officer."

I've heard stories about the CPS. Of children snatched up because they were having a tantrum in a grocery store and couldn't be quieted down in time, children disappeared from a playground when a parent looked away for a moment too long. The families would then be accused of neglect or abuse or—if they were unlucky enough to have no official records of the child's birth—of kidnapping. The child would be taken into state care and adopted out to the highest bidder, sometimes within months. But only the lightest-skinned ones. Only the ones who could pass for white.

"Good for you, what's that got to do with me?"

"I'd like to know your connection to this child."

"And I'd like to know why you're asking."

The woman sighs dramatically, as if I've failed to grasp something obvious. She steps closer to me and pitches her voice low, a tone I guess she thinks is reassuring.

"Look, I don't know how you came into possession of this child, and I'm sure you've formed a bond with her. But we all know childcare is a lot of work. We are offering free adoption and family reunification services to all unaccompanied newcomer minors four years and younger. If you turn her over to us, we'll make sure she finds a good home—and you, as her temporary caregiver, will be generously compensated."

She's not the first person to assume that my light-skinned daughter, with her grey eyes and reddish-blond curls, isn't mine. Nor is she the first person to offer me money for her. She's just the most official.

It's finally my turn at the window. As I step forward, I flash my ID card at the reader on top of her clipboard. It beeps as my biometrics flash onto her screen. Her mouth tightens into a thin line of disapproval as she reads the section listing Nomi as my biological child.

"Thanks for the info, boss lady. But I think I'll keep her."

The woman steps back as if stung. Her look is venomous.

I laugh, deep and rich.

• • • • •

I LOG OFF WITH my last client of the day and decide that I need a walk. A walk or a stiff drink. Working with newcomer patients is always hard. It's not just the traumas that chased them from their homelands, it's the added traumas of adapting to a land that's still struggling with its own wounds. It's not as bad as when I first arrived here thirty years ago. We don't stuff refugees into giant block towers at the edge of town or run them through endless bureaucratic hoops so that they can earn the privilege of belonging. After the Orange Wave brought the first Indigenous-led government to power—miigwetch—all that nonsense went out the window. Relocation still isn't easy, but it can be kind.

A cool spring breeze blows through the bay windows across from me. I like keeping them open to the water as much as I can throughout the year. The craggy seaside of

Newfoundland is nothing like the warm beaches of my New Orleans homeland, but the sea salt air feels familiar all the same. Nomi stirs at my feet and looks up hopefully, his tail thumping softly against the hardwood floor. His shaggy brown coat is starting to shed its winter fullness—there's dog hair everywhere already. I stand and stretch, my joints creaking and popping in protest, and head to the front door, Nomi cheerfully padding behind.

Turns out therapy and sex work aren't all that different. It's all about connection; and I'd always been good at reading people. So when I got that unbelievably large cheque, I decided to start again. No more Memory Store. I went back to school; I moved out of the city and started my own practice. I bought a house up on the coast.

It's been a good life, I reflect as I walk. The path slopes gently downhill and I amble slowly, giving my hips time to loosen up with the exercise. I hold Nomi's leash loosely. The old hound matches my pace, alert but relaxed, beside me.

I stop at the grocery store to grab some fruit—I can never remember what's in season. I'm browsing the freezer aisle when I see a flavour of ice cream I've never tried before. I pick it up without thinking and try to figure out why it's so familiar. It's still in my hands when a young woman comes up to stand beside me.

"Chocolate's my favourite flavour too," she says off-hand.

"It's artificial, you know," I don't even look at her before the words spill out. "Cacao went extinct in 2050."

"I know. It's more about the memories for me. I had

the real stuff once—with my birth mom when I was six."
I turn and take a good look at the woman.

She looks like she's in her thirties. Tall, a good head taller than me, with a strong, sturdy frame. She's light-skinned—the shade my mom would have called "a trick of the light" and my generation called "racially ambiguous." Her eyes are grey, and her reddish-blond hair is plaited into cornrows that end in a froth of curls at the nape of her neck.

"Six years old? You remember that?" I ask skeptically.

"I've got a great memory," she smiles, and something about her gap-tooth grin makes my heart lurch in my chest.

"Do I know you?" I ask because she feels like someone I should know. Something I should remember. But it keeps slipping away from me just out of my reach.

She shakes her head, and her smile turns sad. She asks my name—pronouncing it correctly—and I confirm.

"I'm from the Ministry of Truth and Reconciliation. We're putting together a formal censure of the Cognitive Diagnosis and Recovery Clinics of the late 2040s. Do you know about them?"

"The Memory Stores? Sure, I remember them. They're just about the only thing I do remember these days." I laugh, but there's no humour in it. I've been on anti-dementia medication since I was thirty-five because of that place. I've forgotten more than I could ever hope to know.

"There's evidence that the clinics harvested patient memories in order to claim their children and sell them to the highest bidder. I'm working to gather testimony from former patients. I understand you were one of them. Would you be able to talk with me this week?"

"Happy to. You a lawyer?"

"Bioethicist. I'm part of a research team that's hoping to restore patient's stolen memories."

I nod. Somehow, it seems appropriate that she would be a scientist.

"So where are you now?" she asks.

My mouth moves before I can register what I'm saying. "I'm right here, sugarcube. Always."

Her gap-tooth smile is wide and warm as a summer afternoon.

A FAIR ASSESSMENT

Terese Mason Pierre

MISS ZINNIA'S ANTIQUES AND Vintage shop was located on the eastern edge of Parkdale, on Queen, flanked by an overpriced café and a meek instrument rental store.

I worked there as a part-time appraiser.

My commute was long, but I was grateful. Anything to get away from my fintech roommates, who frequently hosted parties on Saturday nights and spent the next day hungover and useless. I got to the shop at 8:00 a.m. that Sunday, my breath still forming white clouds despite CP24's promise of spring.

The front room was filled with shelves and cabinets housing all manner of old, once-loved valuables—dish sets, jewellery, purses, and more—washed in a soft gold glow when I turned on the lights. By the cash register, on a single tea-stained sheet of paper, Miss Zinnia had written, in her swirling script, two columns: *treasure* and *hope*. Under *treasure*, a list of "new" goods she'd acquired from her long winter sojourns to God-knows-where. Under *hope*, what she thought each item would be worth in Canadian dollars. My job was to verify.

Grabbing the list, I started in the back room, where I found boxes and boxes of Miss Zinnia's carefully wrapped treasures, tagged with bright-orange labels.

This would take me all day.

A wooden table nearly bisected the room; I sat on the side closest to the door. I pushed my coworkers' projects and paperwork to one side of the table, making space for me to work. I opened my leather kit and pulled out my tools: a grimoire the size of my palm; a clay bowl I'd painted pink; two canvas pouches of cemetery soil and salt, and other elixirs necessary for my casting.

In order to determine how to price each item, I'd have to ask the original owner, learn the stories. The customers liked the stories, and so did I. Most importantly, I'd have to find out if any item had its own well of latent magic, which would be detectable regardless of if the spirit came to me when invited. We couldn't sell the cursed items, at least not to ordinary humans. Miss Zinnia had learned this lesson with a set of knives from England—when she was younger, fresh off the plane from Trinidad, the glint of capitalist naïveté bright in her eyes—and she had been wary ever since. Miss Zinnia did some magic too, of course, mostly for basic household chores and quick transport when she wanted to avoid airports. But this kind of work was beyond her skill, so she'd hired me eight years ago.

I filled the clay bowl with warm water and the other required elixirs, and flipped to the correct page in the grimoire. I had memorized the spell long ago, but the book was more of a security blanket. I was experienced, yes, but also self-taught, and mistakes were riskier.

I sprinkled some dirt in as large a circle as I could, then traced that circle with salt. I picked up the first of Zinnia's haul—a China set—and placed it in the centre. I dipped one hand in the water to ground myself and lay the fingers of my other hand on the item. I spoke the spell and felt my body relax into routine, the contours of my voice turning into something old and dark.

The dead, like the living, had complicated feelings about their things.

I learned this the first time I invited a spirit into Miss Zinnia's shop for an appraisal. It was during open hours—my first mistake—and I'd been distracted. I'd held up a denim jacket, dark wash with patches on the shoulders and pockets, and asked the spirit how much this might be worth. My second mistake: not building rapport, despite how inherently weak I knew these connections were. The spirit—a white man, British, in his eighties—had reached over the table as if he could touch the jacket, as if he could take it with him to the hereafter, demanding to know where I'd gotten it. I didn't know where Miss Zinnia had gotten it and told him that, but he grew restless—so restless, he'd tried to inhabit my body, push my own spirit out. That hadn't happened since I started casting in my midteens, and I thought I'd be better by then, at twenty-one.

When I told Miss Zinnia about it, she'd asked if she should hire a second caster for protection—and so I wouldn't be too exhausted—but I'd quickly reassured her I could handle it and it wouldn't happen again.

"Lord, girl, don't be so desperate. I'm not going to fire you," Miss Zinnia had said as we passed a joint back and forth on the bench outside, afterward, while I shook and water streamed from my eyes.

But I'd wanted so badly to be good at this, to be good at anything.

And I was now. I got better at reading the spirits' temperaments, and knowing when it was time to release them. Sometimes the spirits were aggressive or excited to talk to someone—anyone. Sometimes they were confused, having no memory of ever purchasing the item. Sometimes they hated the entire endeavor and asked that I release my bind, not caring at all about their former possessions.

Sometimes we didn't understand each other at all, but that was okay.

•

I CONTINUED MY APPRAISALS for the morning and part of the afternoon, taking breaks so I didn't over-exert myself.

Three times in the morning, I stood outside and listened to the noise of Queen Street until my body returned to equilibrium.

I checked off the items on Miss Zinnia's list, marking in red pen where I thought the price could change, based on what the spirits told me. Today's spirits were mostly from the States and the Caribbean, which meant majority-English speakers. But one was from Brazil, and another French, and my conversation skills were barely passable. I made a note to update my language-learning app.

Thankfully, nobody got hostile and nothing was cursed. The downside to working while the shop was closed was that I was usually alone. I kept a separate notebook with spirits' stories, which I'd later transcribe into a computer for my coworkers to read and integrate into their sales pitches.

At around 3:30 p.m., I'd finished about half of Miss Zinnia's list. I had room for one more in my day, and I'd tackle the rest tomorrow.

I picked up the next item—an incredibly tarnished ring that appeared to be silver, but I couldn't be sure. I placed it inside the dirt-and-salt circle on the table. The ring was small, like a child's, and for a split second, I worried that Miss Zinnia had gotten scammed.

I dipped my hand in the water and invited the spirit into the shop.

A woman appeared in the chair opposite me, her image flat at first, then more substantial. She was young, no more than nineteen or twenty maybe. She had brown skin like me, and from what she wore, it was hard to tell when she died—a long-sleeved cotton shirt buttoned up to her neck, pale and undyed, and a matching headwrap. I imagined she was wearing a skirt too, but I didn't check. No jewellery or makeup. She was small, under five feet, and she wrapped her arms around herself, her gaze trailing around the space. Her eyes were wide with ... not terror, or confusion, but something else.

Spirits didn't need to breathe of course, but I could hear her instinctive breaths as she tried to calm herself.

I began my spiel. "My name is Sarah Baptiste," I said. "I'm a spirit caster. Don't worry, I won't keep you very long. I know this is uncomfortable for you."

Spirits often got cold in our realm and tired easily, or so I'd been told.

I gestured around me with my free hand. "This is Miss Zinnia's Antiques and Vintage shop, in Toronto, Canada. Can you tell me your name?"

The woman—girl?—finished her visual sweep of the room. I watched her gaze settle on many of the larger items of Miss Zinnia's haul, some likely recognizable.

"My name is Ruth," she finally said. She held a hand to her chest, her voice small.

"Ruth?"

"Ruth ... Duncan." She had a Caribbean accent, that much I knew, but I couldn't place the specific island.

I jotted her name in my notebook. The name was

familiar, loosely, like a memory stirred in a breeze. This sometimes happened—one spirit would remind me of a former.

"Where are you from, Ruth?"

"St. David's."

"Oh!" I said. "I've been there! Small world."

"You from there?"

"Uh … my parents are. But I'm from somewhere else. Or I was *born* somewhere else. I was born in Scarborough." I pointed east, as if that made a difference.

Ruth stared at me. I smiled, but she didn't return the gesture. My face warmed. I'd gotten less responsive spirits before, but something about her made me self-conscious.

I cleared my throat and tapped the ring. "Anyway … we've acquired this ring here, and we're hoping you can help us price it properly, since you seem to have a connection to it. It's part of an appraisal process that we do. What can you tell me about it?"

Ruth considered. "It was my wedding ring."

"How old were you when you married?"

She tilted her head up and tapped her chin. "Fifteen. No. Fourteen."

"Oh." I regretted bringing it up. I snuck a glance at her fingers, which were small. Her hands could be a child's hands.

She looked up at me, big brown eyes blinking. "Are you some kind of obeah woman?"

"Not technically. I never learned that specific practice,

sadly. Actually—" I shook my head, cutting myself off. "Never mind. About the ring—"

"What kind of magic you do, Miss Sarah? It's not devil stuff, right?"

"Sarah is fine. And no, it's just ..." But I didn't know how to describe it, the thing that filled my blood and sewed me to the universe. "I learned from books."

"*Books?* What you mean, *books*?"

I frowned. "I bought an old grimoire—spellbook—at an estate sale and started reading for fun. But then it became real, so I kept going."

"Did anyone teach you? Guide you? Someone in your family?"

I gripped my pen. "I had some mentors, not family. No one else in my family does magic, or at least no one alive. I mostly taught myself."

She smiled for the first time. "Good for you."

"Could you tell me a little about your marriage?" I asked quickly, turning the conversation.

Ruth nodded. "Yes. I married Mr. Charles Duncan on June eighth, 1914. He was a butcher. He had more money than my family. We had"—she counted on her fingers—"five children, and the fifth killed me. After a few days. This was when I was twenty. No. Nineteen."

I jotted this down too. "So the ring is valuable. Sentimental, yes?"

"His friend made the ring. Not fancy at all. But it was the nicest thing I owned." She paused, and I could feel her watching me write. "I don't think you'll make much money from this, Miss Sarah. Maybe best to throw it away. Or give it away."

"It's just Sarah. And I can't do that. My manager paid for it."

"Sorry to your mistress."

I wondered if I was wasting my time. Miss Zinnia had written *$140* under *hope* for this item. Should I reduce it? Keep asking Ruth more questions?

"Where did she find it?" said Ruth. "I wanted to give it to my first daughter."

"I don't know. But it might have gone to one of your children regardless."

Her shoulder slumped. "I guess it don't matter now."

The awkwardness I felt earlier returned. "Tell me about your children."

Her eyes lit up. "Diana, Charles Jr., Paul, Thomas, Frederica. I didn't get to spend much time with them, as you know, but I knew they were going to be bright. Charles Jr. was so smart, even as an infant. And Diana was kind. I think she was like you."

I kept quiet. The name Diana Duncan hit hard and sharp in the back of my head like a stone. I set my pen down and picked up the ring again, my other hand still dipped in the water.

"What do you mean she was like me?"

Ruth leaned forward conspiratorially. "I think she could do magic like you. I don't where she learned it—she was five—but there were things that happened around me that could not be explained. Maybe I'm wrong, but I don't think so. I think she could speak to animals. I remember this time she woke up in the middle of the night to tell the crapo to hush, and outside was quieter. Mosquito never bothered her. She helped me pick fruit in the market, and when I cut them open, inside would be more fruit."

"What did you do? What did you say?"

"There was nothing I could do. By the time I really started to see it, I got sick in labour." She shrugged. "And then, you know."

My chest felt cold. "Sorry, where did you say you were from again?"

"St. David's."

All the questions I had formed a steady drip and pooled at the back of my throat, waiting for manifestation. There was no reason for me to keep asking questions about magic. I reminded myself that I had to focus on Miss Zinnia's list and my job. But Ruth said the ring was all but worthless, and she didn't care what happened to it. This was a loss, but I wasn't treating it like that.

I turned the ring in my hand, looking for any clues.

"Something wrong? Your magic not working?"

"It's fine," I said. "The name Diana is familiar."

"Mm. If my mother were here, she would know. She can find anything from a name. You give her somebody's name and she could tell you what parish they were from, what job the family did, everything."

The question was bugging me. "I have a question, about Diana."

"What?"

I pulled one of the few dregs of knowledge I knew. "Did she have a large birthmark on her face, by any chance?"

Ruth's eyes widened. "How do you know that?"

I set the ring down gently, every iota of discomfort rushing into my body and making it hum. I wanted to leave, wanted to release her, but I couldn't. What were the odds? I checked Miss Zinnia's list again. *Where* had she gotten this thing?

"*How do you know that?*" Ruth repeated, when I didn't respond. "Did you bring my child here? Did you talk to her? What did she say?"

"No."

"Then how do you know?"

"Diana Duncan is my great-grandmother."

Ruth looked like she didn't believe me.

I wouldn't believe me either. "I met her in person once, when I was eight. I ended up doing a project on her—interview a family member and write an essay on it, or something. The surnames in our family changed. She married someone named Francis, had my grandmother and six other children. My grandmother was her third, married someone named Douglas, and had my mom and her siblings. My mom kept her last name, but I have my dad's: Baptiste."

Ruth nodded. I knew she was a spirit, but she looked

real, then. "So she is where you get your magic from." She said it like it was an open-and-shut case. "Why you didn't ask her to teach you anything?"

"She died when I was ten. Before I started learning."

"Why you didn't call her here like you called me?"

My cheeks felt hot. "It's not so simple. I ... I don't have anything that belonged to her."

"What about your grandmother? Your mother? No magic there?"

"I told you, no. No one. Just me."

"It can't be just you!"

"Well, *it is*!"

My voice rang out in the empty shop, high and strained. For a moment, no one said anything.

Ruth frowned. "Miss Sarah, I will *not* tolerate—"

I cut her off. "Yeah, I get it, I get it. Sorry." Her tone reminded me too much of my parents, whose house I couldn't wait to escape from, even if it meant roommates.

I could tell she wanted to protest, but she said nothing. Here, in Miss Zinnia's shop, I was ten years her senior. I took some deep breaths.

"Apparently, my mom tried to convince her to come to a long-term care home, but she wanted to stay in St. David's. Not sure it would have made a difference lengthening her life. She was healthy and active to the end. Ninety."

Ruth leaned forward, the hint of a hopeful smile on her face. "What was she like?"

"I only spent one day with her. I don't remember much."
"Anything is better than nothing."

•

I LEARNED OF MY great-grandmother's existence two hours before I met her. My family spent March break in St. George's, and we drove around the island in my parents' all-wheel-drive Jeep. They'd dumped my brother and me at Diana's house in St. David's on their way to see friends in Grenville, farther north. I had no idea where these places were at the time, but I didn't protest the shepherding. I loathed when I had to step out of their air-conditioned vehicle and into the blistering heat, or worse, the rain.

Diana's house was yellow, a colour I was embarrassed by, but I could admit, even at eight, that it was a me problem. Secretly, I was impressed that a great-anything of mine was still alive.

The first thing I noticed about Diana was that she was popular. Over the course of my nine-hour visit, there was a constant parade of people in and out of her home. Most left gifts and stayed for conversation, and their speech was so accented, so warbled with laughter, I couldn't understand what they were saying. Her neighbourhood was active, community consistently lurking around every corner. I didn't know if I preferred it to Toronto's iciness, which I gleaned sharply, even as a child.

While I was there, my great-grandmother tried to educate

me. She handed me her copy of *The Student's Companion*, a book, orange and sweet-smelling from aged pages. I did not come all the way here for more school, so she gave up, but I did spend an hour flipping through it, lying on her bed with the fan in my face, while my brother watched television and chased stray cats and snakes around the yard. The book was filled with a brand of trivia and general knowledge I didn't think I had a use for, but my favourite part ended up being the section on collective nouns for animals. I learned that a group of starlings was called a "murmuration," a group of hippopotamuses, a "bloat."

Diana asked me, some time later in the lull between visitors, to sit outside with her on the bench in her backyard. I was confused but did as I was told, heaving myself down dramatically. She held my hand. Her skin was soft and papery-smooth. I couldn't remember if she was wearing a ring. Whenever I tried to start a conversation, she pressed her finger to her lips, then to her ear. The wind sounded like rain through the palms, which also sounded like cars over gravel; the chickens and goats of her neighbours—and her neighbours too—had their own meandering, musical tête-à-têtes; the dogs ran and barked in the street; Diana's breathing was wispy but steady, and my own was loud with barely contained verve; we were too far away from the ocean to hear it, but from her house, we could see it in all its glorious, cerulean danger. We named all the sounds we heard and the things we knew were there but that we could not hear. I asked her if she did this every day.

"I talk to a lot of folks," she said. "Some here, some elsewhere. Listening helps, not speaking helps."

We sat quietly for a few more minutes before I grew restless again.

I had been wearing shorts because of the heat, and I could tell she wasn't pleased about it. She pointed to a mark on my exposed thigh and asked if I had burned myself. I told her it was a mark I'd had since I was born. She pointed to an identical one on her face, which was a half-shade lighter than her skin—something I had noticed immediately upon meeting her but did not bring up.

It was the most excited I'd seen her, and her eyes welled up, as if she'd been waiting for this moment her entire life. She did not explain further. She held out her fist and asked me what my favourite flower was. I said tulip, and she when she opened her palm, a tulip bud appeared. Inside the tulip bud was a second, smaller, tulip bud—out of place, but perfect.

I'd thought this was a cool trick, and did not ask how she'd done it, remembering what every single birthday party magician had told me prior. When I saw her later in the day, she seemed brighter and more relieved, thanking her neighbours effusively, laughing a little louder than before.

Later, by the time I thought to reach out for her, she was gone.

•

RUTH LISTENED. HER FACE was still, but her hands, gripping the table, betrayed her desire to learn more. She stared at the ring again.

"And you don't know if she was wearing it?"

"I don't. I'm sorry. Maybe she was, but ... I don't know."

Ruth sat back. She said nothing for a long time, and for a while, the only sound in the room was the large grandfather clock in the corner. "You said you didn't remember anything, but I thought that was detailed, everything you said."

"Maybe it's your presence," I said, half-heartedly trying for a joke. I felt the connection straining, and the needle of a migraine at the base of my skull. "But I'm sorry anyway. I know that's not what you were hoping for."

"No, no. I wanted to know something carried forward, you know?" She shivered. "But there's you, so I suppose I have my answer."

I nodded, uneasy. Her words were innocent enough, but for me they carried a familiar, imaginary challenge, and I hoped I wouldn't fail.

"Are you *sure* you can't call on Diana?" Ruth asked. "She could teach you."

"I told you I don't have anything of hers."

"What about that book?"

"I ... I lost it a long time ago." This was only half-true; it was lost in my parent's basement somewhere under mountains of art supplies, tools, decorations, and albums.

"Nothing is lost," Ruth said, reading my face. "Look again."

"I could try."

"And could you ... invite *me* again? I feel sleepy. I want to ask you things, but I don't know what."

My chest squeezed. "Of course."

"Thank you, Miss Sarah. I will wait for your call."

I cut the connection and watched her fade like steam in the air. I lifted my hand from the water, and a crushing nausea hit me all at once, my vision blurring. When I returned from the bathroom, my limbs heavy, I saw the ring still sitting in the middle of the table. I left it there as I deliberated, as I packed up my things and tidied the space and prepared to brave the Toronto wind chill again.

At the last second, I slid the ring into my pocket. It was more than I'd hoped.

PEAK DAY

Suyi Davies Okungbowa

8:00 a.m.

WELCOME TO EVERYTHING CO. You applied for this role yourself? Solid. So you already know what we do here. No time to waste; doors open in an hour. I'll show you around, then to your workstation and your task for the day.

Hey, look at me—don't look outside. Ignore them.

Just to confirm, your implant is working fine? Tested and all? Because we can't have that malfunctioning. It's Peak Day. You know what that is? Solid. We can't have Peak Day without you. Today, more than any other day, we have a singular purpose: to understand everything the customer wants before they want it. We must anticipate their needs and deliver to them what they want before they know they want it. That's how we serve here at Everything.

I said stop looking outside.

That, you can look at. Magnificent, eh? I'm sure you're

wondering what's inside. Don't worry, everybody wonders what's under that dome. Want to guess? Here are the top three things new joiners always say: a supercomputer, banks of servers, a secret weapon. Unfortunately, it's none of those things! But I'll let you in on a little secret. It's also *all* of those things! Ha!

No, I've not seen it myself. No one has. All our fulfillment centres have one, but no one knows what's in it. Even prenotes like you who get to work with it never know.

More on that later. Come, join the morning assembly.

8:32 a.m.
All right, did you catch everything? Solid. Any questions?

Your station? Up there. Let's walk over.

I hear you're still a bit dizzy. Aftereffects of the surgery, is it? Well, I don't know what to do about that. I'll have to check in with my director. I hear this all stabilizes once you put on the helmet, so maybe once you get to working, you'll feel better.

I know I'm prying—and I'm not supposed to pry—but is it true you were almost dead before we stepped in? Aneurysm, was it? Wow. Can't believe we're literally out there hijacking death! Not only pulling you from its jaws with proprietary tech, but also giving you a job using that same proprietary tech. Yes, yes, I know it's to repay the costs, but, you know. Death or work—I know which I'd choose.

Prying again, but how much time do you have on your bond? Know what, don't answer that. Against policy.

Here's your workstation. It's all very simple—this is the helmet, these are your three keys. Helmet runs database scans on an ongoing loop, filtering for useful datapoints, and your job is to sift through the datapoints presented and match them.

Helmet on—here, let me show you.

Solid. Now, green key here is for when you see an audience datapoint that matches a stock datapoint. What does that mean? That a potential customer may want or will soon want something. The dome will know and show you. Not in your visor, no—neurosignals. In your brain. Then you "see," if you catch my meaning.

Okay, so use the green key to approve, and the floor techs will do the rest. Oh, yeah, they just pressure the stock datapoints against the audience datapoint until they collide. *Collide* is how we say *completed sale* here in these parts.

Solid. Now, yellow key is for when you're unsure if the datapoints match. If you use that, the datapoints will be recycled and presented to you again until you're sure whether or not they match. Red key is for when you're *sure* they don't match. But let me warn you right now: do not use red, ever. Red says there's a malfunction in the dome and therefore it's giving you wrong results. There's never a malfunction in the dome. There *cannot* be a malfunction in the dome on Peak Day. In fact, if there's a malfunction today, it will be you. I suggest you scan your brain implant before considering the red key.

You don't have a scanner? Why? Can't afford it? Well. What can I say?

Anyway, if there's a malfunction, it's you.

I'll go up to my station right there—look where I'm pointing; I told you to stop looking outside. I'm going there now to push a few trial datapoints to you, see if everything is working fine. We have less than a quarter hour before doors open.

Oh, one last thing: you know your implant is remotely controlled, right? They can turn it on or off at any time. Not *me*—I don't have that ability; I'm just a floor manager. But if your results—which they receive in real-time—if your results are not up to par, you get time added to your bond. And then, if they please, they can shut off your implant anytime. And you know what happens when they shut it off, right?

Solid.

8:55 a.m.

Can you hear me? Just double-checking the intercom over here.

One thing: many prenotes say they experience a bit of vertigo when the first rush of datapoints come in. It may happen to you once doors open, but don't be alarmed. It's just the dome and your implant establishing connection and your brain getting used to that.

Still dizzy? Let's hope you don't get that vertigo.

No, I'm sorry, you can't sit. Look around. Do you see any chairs? We don't sit here at Everything Co. But don't worry, you'll get used to it. I've been floor manager for over a decade and I've stood through all my shifts.

All right, look alive. Here it comes.

9:02 a.m.
Doing all right there, buddy? No vertigo? Only a little? Solid.

See that number in the top right corner of your visor? That's your productivity value. It's based on the collision success rate that comes from your approvals, and then applied against your bond. Positive values—high collision rates—reduce your bond. Negative values—low collision rates—increase your bond. So don't just go approving everything and anything. You'll only be hurting yourself.

9:23 a.m.
Buddy, you will need to stop looking outside. They have your visor feed, you know? They can see everything.

10:11 a.m.
Excellent work there, buddy. Yes, I know your name is not "buddy," but let's use that for now, shall we? We'll see if you last long enough for me to use your name, or if you'll be like previous prenotes.

11:07 a.m.
Break is at noon, a sharp thirty minutes. Small note of warning: do *not* attempt to mingle with the other workers.

You are not like them, they are not like you. You have a special role here. Focus on that.

We can take lunch together, if that'll help you keep to time.

12:10 p.m.
First days are hard, yeah? Okay, here's a bit of a salvo. You can ask three questions. I'll give you three answers as best I can without getting into trouble.

I can't tell you how many departments we have, but let me tell you this: many of them are just like ours. That is, they have only one or two workers. Everything else is automated. If you stretch your neck now and look at that floor, how many people can you find? Exactly. Now count the automatons. Exactly.

Outside? Ah, well, that's unfortunately an anti–Peak Day rally. You must've seen one before joining us, right? They're all over every media, everyday, all the time. Each Peak Day, they gather there outside, rallying against us, accusing us of silly things—their favourite label is *techno-capitalist slavers*. Ha! Imagine that. Policy is just to ignore them, which is why I keep asking you to not look outside.

Why would you ask that? How are previous prenotes any of your business? You're the current prenote. Focus on that.

Look, we're done here. Better hurry up and go relieve yourself. You won't get another opportunity before end of day.

1:02 p.m.
What is it?

Flashes? What do you mean *flashes*?

Wait, I'm coming down.

1:04 p.m.
I've never heard of that before. Are you making this up?

Describe them, then. Describe these "flashes."

I see. And you don't quite remember these faces you're seeing? Then how do you know they're your friends or family? Okay, so you don't know. How does this concern me exactly?

Buddy, if you can't remember your people's names or faces, that's a you problem.

The headaches—how severe? Well, you better take your meds, because I can see your productivity points already dropping.

You don't have meds? Why? You couldn't aff—can you afford *anything*?

Want my advice? Find a way to solve this and get back to work immediately. You can mess up your productivity all you want, but if you mess up mine, I swear to god—

What the *fuck*?

1:38 p.m.
Can you imagine this bullshit? How did they get access to our fire alarm system? Wasting a whole half hour mustering out there, forced to listen to the disgusting nonsense they're

shouting. It's what they wanted, wasn't it? They don't even care they're being arrested. Idiots.

All right, here's the debrief room. You may have a seat.

No, I'm not kidding. This is the one room in this establishment where you can sit.

Okay, now listen, there's one reason for this room, and it's this: this is the silence room.

By that, I mean that all the things you want to say, you say them in here, right now. Let it all out. All you have seen out there, the stories you're itching to get back home and tell your people—this is your opportunity to open your mouth and tell those stories. And then you walk out of these four walls, and you forget those stories. You forget everything you have seen and heard outside. You leave it all here in this room, and you never speak of it again.

You remember your bond? You remember the nondisclosure that was a part of it?

Solid. Now, talk.

Talk, I said.

Nothing to say? Are you sure? Nothing about the slogans? The "Boycott Everything Co!" or "Strike!" or "Unionize!"? No?

Okay, let me be more direct: when those cameras approached you, they asked some questions and said some things. For instance, they called you, and I quote, "A wilting bag of worker flesh, squeezed by the Everything Co. Prenote Program even in death." Of our Superhero Worker campaign, they said, "You are not a telepathic superhero;

you are a walking zombie." And, and … these are just too disturbing, I can't keep reading.

I just want you to know: you are not a wilting bag of worker flesh or a walking zombie. You are a treasured part of the Everything Co. family. You must know that. I also want you to know that the moment you leave this room, it is expected that you never repeat a word of anything you have heard in here or out there to anyone, ever. Understand? Solid.

Nothing to say? Ah, the headache and dizziness. Back to your station, then. You've already lost one productivity hour. I can put in word for it to be forgiven, but only this once, just because it wasn't your fault. But don't be expecting this from me every time you fall short.

2:22 p.m.
Buddy, not to interrupt but I just wanted to let you know that your productivity hour's been forgiven. You'll see it update in your visor soon.

Another thing: about those flashes? I ran it up the chain and they told me that, yes, you in fact have a family. They're very grateful to Everything Co. for saving you and are excited to welcome you back when your bond is done. So, yeah, that's … that.

No, I'm sorry, you'll have to hold it. No breaks until end of day.

3:14 p.m.
Worse? What do you mean *worse*?

Wait, I'm coming down.

3:17 p.m.
What are you doing? You can't just—*stop*—don't take it off!

Ohh, I get it. You're trying to ruin my life, aren't you? You're trying to ruin my life! Please put on the helmet. It's Peak Day, don't you understand? You need me to kneel down and beg? Okay, I'm on my knees. Please, I beg you. It's Peak Day. I have a family too, you understand? It's Peak Day! We need peak collisions! Fifty percent of annual collisions come from Peak Day!

Please, put on the helmet.

Please. You want me to say your name? I will say it. Just put on the helmet.

You can do it. You can. The headaches, the dizziness, they will go away. You just need to prenote more. The more you do it, the more you get used to it. In the back of your mind, like breathing. You don't feel it anymore.

No, not like being *numb*—are you even listening to me?

Stop. Where are you going? Come back!

Come b—

Buddy? Buddy?

Medical! Get us Medical!

4:49 p.m.
Yes, sir, I understand. Yes, I do. Yes, I'm aware it's Peak

Day. Yes, sir, I know what happens when we don't meet peak collisions.

No problem, sir.

Yes, I've sent out the usual rounds: station decommission, record purge, presence scrub, implant uninstall. Yes, no family or friends, confirmed.

Well, sir, I can't control footage that doesn't exist within our systems. Perhaps someone else can scour external media to find stuff from our brief time outside. I don't know what to say. I'm only a floor manager.

Well, *was*, so.

Doors are closing, sir. I'll take my leave now. I appreciate the generous package. I've enjoyed my time at Everything. Thank you.

HALLELUJAH HERE AND ELSEWHERE
francesca ekwuyasi

1. Here

HALLELUJAH IS A RAVENOUS woman; whatever she eats, she devours thoroughly. Fat mangoes are reduced to moon-shaped seeds scraped so clean that streaks of fuzzy white fibres lie flat in the tracks carved by her teeth. She speaks with a stutter, which often has the effect of making her seem timid, until you witness her command a room of students. Her father, Patrice, calls her by doubling the fourth syllable in her name—Lulu. He calls her every Sunday at 4:00 p.m. to ask if she happened to make it to the morning Mass, or to remind her that she still has time to make it to the evening Mass.

Her lover, Tafa, only calls her by the first two syllables of her name—Halle—when they try to refrain from cruelly tearing each other apart during their rare but heated arguments, or when they rip each other open in desperately gorgeous ways during their lovemaking. Otherwise, Tafa calls her *Babe* or *Guapa* or some other tender term of endearment.

Hallelujah insists that her students call her in full proclamation, *Hallelujah!*, which she prefers. Or Ms. Mamadou, which she finds acceptable. At twenty-nine, she is one of the youngest postdocs in the biology department of Saint Agnes University. And even though she has instructed classes since midway through her Master's degree, she feels that she must prove her authority to teach, as if a doctorate in her field is insufficient.

Hallelujah developed her stutter suddenly at the age of eight. Her tongue began to stumble around consonants when she witnessed the aftermath of her mother, Genevieve's, first attempt at ending things. She woke from an afternoon nap to find her mother in the bathtub, fully dressed, limbs jerking in violent convulsions, all the while foaming at the mouth.

Genevieve had been warding off something dark since she was an early teen, something that seemed to require blood or some other equally vital part of her. That day—in a moment of clarity that one might also call sheer exhaustion—she thought, *Why not?* She'd only gone to the bathroom to urinate, but she decided it was as good a place as any. So, she gulped down the entire contents of five pill bottles. Her eyes had just started rolling back, and her limbs involuntarily jumped when she heard the soft plodding of her daughter's footsteps approaching the bathroom. She regretted only that Hallelujah would have to see. She failed that day but would succeed a handful of years later, on the very day that Hallelujah, in a fit of rage at having been scolded for singing too loudly, wrote in her diary, *I wish she would just shut up and die.*

In a frenzy, after she learned of her mother's death, she tore the page out of the diary and shoved it into her mouth, letting her warm saliva soften the stiff paper before chewing quickly, thoroughly, until she swallowed the starchy paste. Only to vomit violently when she found out that her father had been in the car when her mother decided to drive it straight into the mouth of a moving truck transporting pineapples and oranges to the Nigerian border. Her father survived, but the head injury he suffered from the impact was so severe that both his eyes were badly damaged and had to be removed entirely. He also lost his memory of what occurred. He still refers to the incident as an accident, and Hallelujah never tells him that it was not so.

For one semester in the fourth year of her doctorate, Hallelujah taught an undergraduate course, Principles of Ecology. She felt the prickly warmth of her most diligent student's coy gaze lingering on her face throughout the semester. The student was Tafa, and she was intent on completing the degree she had half-heartedly pursued for the better part of a decade. Tafa was entering her early thirties with some quiet success as a novelist. And though she was finally able to afford to take courses without any need for a day job, she suspected that she would never grow accustomed to surviving without one. So she kept a few hours selling the work of her favourite authors at a second-hand bookstore in the North End—a damp and narrow second-floor shop sweetened by the honeyed-yeast aroma from a Cantonese bakery just below it.

Tafa was taken with Hallelujah right away, first by her name. *Who the fuck is named Hallelujah?* she thought and chuckled as Hallelujah stood before the class introducing herself.

(She would hear the story later, learn that while Hallelujah was forming in utero, her mother honestly hadn't decided if she dared to ask the spirit of her daughter to take flesh form and suffer being alive. She believed that the child's will to live lightened her burden. For her, it felt near euphoric to be purposeful. They'd already picked names: her father named her for his late mother, Mariatou, and her mother named her Joanna for her late twin. But when she pushed her out in the freshly scrubbed bathtub of their duplex in Porto Novo, she screamed "Hallelujah" for the end of the pain, for praise that she had survived it. Patrice held the bloody, slippery infant. As they cleaned her, he blubbered through his tears, "Hallelujah, indeed.")

Second, by her stutter, which was mild but noticeable and, to Tafa, deeply endearing. She too has an impediment in her speech, a lisp that goes mostly unnoticed but reveals itself more boldly in direct proportion to her exhaustion or intoxication. Third, something only mildly seismic, like knee-buckling desire, or chemistry, or lust, or the longing to belong to someone who moved like Hallelujah.

Tafa waited until the semester ended before "coincidentally" bumping into Hallelujah at the dimly lit blues bar by the waterfront that she knew Hallelujah frequented to watch her father play the saxophone in a four-piece jazz band named Butter.

In bed, a handful of weeks after they met at the bar, Tafa reached across Hallelujah for a joint on her bedside table and asked, "You want to get a bit high before I fuck you?"

They were fully clothed and tangled together on top of the covers.

"No," Hallelujah shook her head, her lips tingled from having just been bitten.

"You don't want to?" Tafa asked again.

"Not right now," Hallelujah answered.

"What would you like to do right now?"

"Whatever you want."

Tafa chuckled softly, "I'm *very* open to any number of things; I want to know what *you* want to do."

"Undress me," Hallelujah requested in a firm tone.

Tafa smiled, "You want to be bossy?"

"Stop talking," Hallelujah smiled back, her eyes already sleepy half-moons of desire. "Undress me."

Tafa obeyed. They fucked loud.

•

IT'S BEEN TWO YEARS since, and Tafa is in the shower. They are preparing to attend the launch party of her third novel, titled *Endurance*, a speculative fiction about a shy androideity who must confront her wrathful creators to keep her planet from being destroyed by their careless wars. Tafa wants Hallelujah to join her in the bathroom, but sometimes, after fucking, Hallelujah wants to be alone. She needs a moment to listen to the song of her body and, if necessary, remind herself that she chose whatever pleasure she took. That she was willing, eager even, with what she gave.

So Hallelujah is alone in the living room; she is lying on the cold floor, and her nerves are still dancing from the gentle roars of climax. She looks up and sees a tear, a small rip in the air, about five feet from her face. It is nearly imperceptible, but for the delicate rays of light that shine through to cast a small oily pool of colours on the brown wood of the living-room floor. She has seen this before; yes, she saw it the first time she was in Tafa's place—now their home—she saw it again as they walked across the MacDonald Bridge, but even before then, as a girl in Lokossa, she saw ...

(... perhaps you should know this: Hallelujah has a fury inside her that will consume everything if allowed. But it is merely brittle, poorly tempered glass. Should it shatter, all you'll find in its place is a wound that wants.

During the *incidents* with that uncle in Lokossa, where she had to live while her father recovered, glass-eyed and silent, she clawed at the air, begging with the full force of her blood that it would tear open and take her elsewhere. There were moments when she saw it begin to ripple and shimmer, the wear before the tear. She would never reveal this to her father because she was sure that he would kill the man, and she would prefer to do it herself. Even with all the years that have passed, she would still very much like to see that uncle suffer immensely. Fuck, she would like to taste his blood.

As a teenager, Hallelujah never acted out with her father; it all went inward in the nourishment she denied herself. She grew so thin in those first few winter months in Nova Scotia, so cold. Eventually, her father threatened to force her into treatment, but it was unnecessary. She'd been visited in a dream. A somebody or something that possessed her own face and her mother's voice as it furiously whispered, "Why should you starve when that vile man feasts? Or you think you were the only child from which he gorged himself?"

So she ate.

She eats.

She feeds herself whatever she fancies. She reaches out for help when the fury slips to reveal a sea of sadness too deep to traverse alone. Yet that shimmer, the tear in the air, is here for her now.)

She smiles at the rip, sure that her mind is swiftly unravelling; she says, "You're l-late, and I'm s-safe now."

Yet, she puts the tip of her right forefinger into the tear

without thinking about it too much, and it disappears into the space between. She tugs gently to see if the air will move, and it does. It grows wider around her finger, so she pushes farther until her whole palm, her whole hand, her shoulders, her head, and her entire self goes through.

2. *Elsewhere*

On the Other Side of the torn air, everything is a slightly altered reflection of her own side. The living room is nearly identical, but the round Adire rug in its centre is maroon. It should be indigo. Not should, maybe was …?

Hallelujah feels dizzy. Her head is spinning as though she's been spun fast on a merry-go-round. She tries to still her vision by focusing on the rug that is the wrong colour. She thinks her disorientation must be normal, but even that seems outrageous. There cannot be a "normal" for this.

She looks back to see that the tear is still there. It's larger—ripped open wider by her body—yet still barely perceptible. She wouldn't believe it if she hadn't just done it.

Moving through the room on unsteady feet, she finds more subtle differences: the box of framed photographs is white instead of light brown and the people in the pictures are of her, Tafa, and her father, but also not. There is a picture of Patrice and Tafa smiling wide at her. She picks it up and peers closer. Patrice's eyes are open. That can't be right. Patrice's eyes had to be taken out after the accident. Hallelujah has seen the sunken flesh, blotchy pink and red under his eyelids. She doesn't have to scan the photo too long to see that Tafa is also different. She appears more angular and broader in the shoulders. *Where is Tafa?!*

Hallelujah needs to share this wildness with Tafa. She rushes toward the bedroom to find her—no, them—sitting naked on the edge of their unmade bed, their dusk skin glistening. Tafa is holding a syringe in their right hand and wiping the outer part of their thigh with their left.

"Taf, shit is so w-weird right now!"

"What's wrong?" Tafa asks.

"I th-think I'm dreaming."

"Please?" Tafa asks and hands her the syringe.

Hallelujah looks at it blankly for a moment, and then again, a memory falls in; she sinks to her knees beside this Tafa and deftly pierces the skin of their thigh with the needle. She hasn't ever done this before, but she has also done it quite frequently over the past two years. She takes a deep inhale, and it becomes even more apparent from the smell that is so close to the same but just one note off, one note too sweet where there should be musk; this is not her Tafa. She sees for the first time that this Elsewhere Tafa has two mirroring mastectomy scars on their chest.

Tafa touches Hallelujah's shoulder to get her attention; they hold each other's gaze, and Tafa frowns and strokes the shiny scar on Hallelujah's chin, asking, "Are you okay?"

Hallelujah smiles and nods. She sees now that Elsewhere Tafa's hair is wound into thin locs, thinner than her Tafa's, and they fall down to their elbows in wavy tendrils.

"Your father will be here in a sec," Tafa says. "You ready?"

Hallelujah nods yes because one of three things is happening:

1. Her mind has, rather suddenly, found a new path upon which to wander;
2. She's been dreaming all her life and has just now awoken; or
3. She really did wriggle through a rip in the air in the living room.

Regardless of the three options, she is starting to wonder if there is this other Tafa, as evidenced by the person before her at the moment, and another Patrice, who, according to the photograph in the living room, still has his sight. Then where is the other Hallelujah?

(In fact—a fact that Hallelujah had missed in her disorientation while passing through the split in the air—the Other Hallelujah passed through at the precise moment. They had ventured through the same space simultaneously, their minds unable to reconcile the aberration, so that neither of them saw the other. At the precise moment that Hallelujah wonders about her Other self, the Other self wonders about her as well.)

As promised, Patrice is there within five minutes. Hallelujah meets him at the door with her heart in her throat, pounding so that she cannot speak when she sees him standing at the threshold with a cane in his right hand

and his eyes open. Hallelujah looks into the deep brown of her father's eyes and silent tears fill her own. His face is warm, heavy, and covered in a thin layer of cold sweat when he lets it rest between her hands. She looks and looks. She hasn't seen them since she was a child. But he cannot see her, you know, because many years ago, he suffered a brain injury that took his sight away when his wife nearly killed them both by driving their car straight into the concrete wall of their compound. He cannot see his daughter, but he knows her by the rhythm of her gait, and by her smell—although she smells a tad foreign, perhaps a new perfume.

They embrace; he is less yielding than her own Patrice; he pulls his arms away from her abruptly and asks, "Ça va, Lulu? Qu'est-ce qui se passe?"

"Nothing Papa, ça va toi?" It takes her a moment, but when his gaze fails to follow her movements, she realizes that he is still blind, or was always blind, or is also blind. Everything inside her body is quaking to ask, *Where is Maman?* Instead, she bites her tongue.

"Good, good, I hope you are ready. We cannot be late."

"Late for wha—" Then, again, a memory clicks into place. This Other Tafa is a filmmaker; they have a screening tonight.

"I'm ready. Let me just tell Tafa that you're here," she lies and leaves her father—no, she leaves Elsewhere Patrice in the living room. She rushes to the bedroom, where Tafa is doing up the buttons on a stiff white shirt.

She offers up a shaky smile, "My father is here."

Tafa says, "I'm nervous."

Hallelujah shakes her head, "Don't worry."

She bites back the instinct to reach for Tafa and kiss their forehead. Her self-restraint is in vain because Tafa reaches out and pulls her close. They cover her mouth with a kiss that tells Hallelujah that it is, in fact, a stranger on her lips. That fact sends thrilling ripples of yearning through her gut.

"I have to change," she says as she pulls away. She is wearing the same oversized T-shirt she had on when she slid her body through the tear. She looks through the closet, where Elsewhere Hallelujah's clothes are hung in neat, colour-coded rows smelling of cedar. She selects a tailored navy-blue jumpsuit with a tapered hem that stops just before her ankles and fits snugly on her soft body.

Steam from Tafa's shower still clings to the smooth surfaces in the bathroom; Hallelujah splashes cold water on her face and stares her foggy reflection in the eye. With a half-smile curving her lips and utter bewilderment knotting her eyebrows, she mutters to herself, "You are *actually* an imposter right now."

From the living room, Patrice shouts, "On doit y aller!"

•

TAFA'S FILM SCREENS AT the public library. The auditorium is overflowing with bodies, and people are seated on the steps and the floor by the doors.

Hallelujah is in awe of the film; she is drowned by the same feeling that engulfed her when she read her Tafa's novel and essay collection. She squeezes Elsewhere Tafa's hand and beams with pride that she has no right to claim.

•

"WE'VE BEEN FIGHTING A lot; I'm sorry," Tafa says.

They slipped out of the auditorium just as soon as the Q&A session ended and cabbed to Blanca, a rooftop restaurant in the North End. The place has live jazz. Patrice is already perched on the bench closest to the stage, tapping his foot, shaking his head in rhythm to the drums' giddy beat.

The evening breeze dances warm through the poofy halo of Hallelujah's hair; she strokes Tafa's face and says nothing. The memories that are not really hers grow clearer the longer she stays.

Tafa says, "You're weird." She leans back and squints at Hallelujah. "Is your hair different?"

Hallelujah shakes her head and shrugs. She exhales in relief as the rest of their party joins them and they move to a bigger table in the middle of the restaurant. Soon, they are a raucous group, talking loudly and over each other, but Hallelujah is fixated on Tafa. They are different, but the quickening pull of her body to theirs is familiar. She places her hand on their thigh, wondering if it would be twisted should she end up in bed with this Tafa. She plants light kisses on their arm, barely participating in the conversation. She is fixated on Elsewhere Tafa; maybe it's the mezcal cocktails she's been throwing back between bites of piquant smoked chicken wings, perhaps it's the fact that she's done an impossible thing.

Patrice, who has joined them at the table, touches a firm hand to Hallelujah's shoulder.

"Ma petite, faut que je rentre, je suis fatigué, hein?"

"Pas de souci, Papa, viens, je te dépose," she says, and to Tafa, "I'll take my father home, but I'll come back here, okay?"

"I'll come with you," Tafa replies.

"No, stay here, enjoy your celebration. I won't be long."

Hallelujah hails them a taxi and settles in the backseat beside her father, his white cane folded and resting between them.

"Ça va, Papa? T'as kiffé ta soirée?" She takes his hand and holds it to her chest, to the flat just beneath her collarbone. But this Elsewhere Patrice is a harder man. He is stiffened by the gesture.

"Ah oui! Le film était vraiment intéressant à voir. Tafa, il gère!"

She wants to ask about her mother—no, she wants to ask about Elsewhere Genevieve—but there is no need, because the memories that are not truly her own flood her suddenly, and she remembers:

Elsewhere Patrice is a harder man than his counterpart on Hallelujah's side because he holds tight to the belief that his wife left one Christmas holiday on the South Shore.

The Christmas only two years after the "accident" that left him blind, they flew the seventeen hours to Nova Scotia. It was Hallelujah's first time in her mother's country, and it seemed nothing could breathe warmth into her and stave off the December cold. They'd flown into Halifax, and Genevieve drove them through frosty roads and picturesque snow-laden pines on the way to Lunenburg, telling them that it was named the Christmas tree capital of the world for all the balsam fir trees and their sweet forest scent. A quiet time of year, they'd stayed in a bright-red cottage sitting high on a hill that rolled down to the wild, thrashing ocean. They'd spent most of the holiday in woolen layers around the vintage cast iron, wood-burning stove, eating fruitcake and peppery chicken soup.

Elsewhere Genevieve was not close to her parents, so they'd visited the yellow house in which she grew up for only a few hours on Christmas Eve. A timid two-storey house with narrow stairs, built at a time when people were smaller, so even as a teenager, Elsewhere Hallelujah felt comically large in her grandparents' home. In those few hours, her maternal grandparents cooed at her, told her how happy they were to meet her finally, and expressed an open sentimentality that Elsewhere Hallelujah couldn't trust because it seemed to come too easy and after too little time. She'd felt uneasy there, and so had Elsewhere Patrice. He'd vividly remembered the hard lessons forced on him, as a Black African man—with an accent heavily inflected with Fon and French when he'd lived in those parts over fifteen years prior. And as a blind man, it filled every open pocket of space inside him with dread.

Her grandparents told Elsewhere Hallelujah she was pretty like her mother. They poked at her afro. They showed her pictures of her mother as a child—an only child with pouting pink lips and curly red hair, frowning at being photographed. And some of her beaming, just beaming with a feverish intensity and impossibly big and toothy smile, blurry from vibrating in her own excitement. Even as a child, Hallelujah recognized the frozen flicker in the photographed child's eyes. A unique vibration that her mother synced into sometimes: a high climb of intense, energetic joy that could last days but was always destined to burst and pour down in an agonizing descent that burned everyone around her. On the drive away from her childhood home that Christmas Eve, Elsewhere Genevieve began that steep climb. It tinged that Christmas and the days that followed in a euphoric haze; they cooked, baked, danced, and sang in that red cabin. When it snowed a thick carpet of fluffy white on the day before New Year's Eve, Genevieve brought out a bright-blue plastic toboggan and taught Hallelujah how to sled fast and free down the steep powder-covered hill outside their cabin.

On the night of New Year's Eve, just three hours before twelve, Genevieve drove them the hour and a half to Peggy's Cove so that they could watch and listen to the New Year's Day fireworks illuminate the lighthouse at midnight. Wind ripped violently through their jackets in sharp, cold, and bitter howls when they arrived. Hallelujah worried that her father would slip on the icy boulders, but Genevieve was in a blissful frenzy.

"I'll be his guide," she'd said in the darkness.

Hallelujah felt frustration, like acid reflux, climb her tight throat. She replied, "Papa cannot swim. Also, it's too cold."

"Of course, he can swim," Genevieve retorted. "Don't be stupid, come on." She tugged at the nylon of her husband's windbreaker.

"Maman, stop it, you're being crazy!" Elsewhere Hallelujah hadn't meant to shout it. She hadn't meant for her words to tumble out so caustic.

She was frightened by the vastness of the dark ocean, of the hunger with which its crashing waves lapped at the slick, massive rocks around them. She was worried that she couldn't trust her mother's judgment at that moment. None of that kept Elsewhere Genevieve's face from contorting into a mask of hurt that melted quickly to scorn. She raised her eyebrows and curled her lips in a soulless sneer.

"Fine then," she said, her voice hard. "Let's go home."

Hallelujah was primed to apologize, to beg that they stay and watch the fireworks as planned. But her father searched for her hand and, attempting to dissolve the tension with some cheer, said, "Come on, my darlings. Let us do the fireworks, drink this hot cocoa, and go back to our warm cabin."

But his wife stayed blank—her elation had burst—until

he reached for her hand and cooed, "Come now, sweet Gené ..."

In the warmth of the car, they listened to Dr. Alban's "Guess Who's Coming to Dinner" and watched the burst of glitter in the inky sky. They sang, "Carolina don't run, run, run around," and sat awash in eruptions of light as they drank hot chocolate from a large stainless steel thermos bottle. They embraced and said "Happy New Year" to each other, praying for a prosperous and safe year to come.

Hallelujah believed her mother had forgiven her, but by the next day, she'd disappeared.

No one knew the precise moment of her disappearance, but just after 4:00 a.m., Hallelujah dreamed that her mother plunged feet first into the vast dark water. Her descent was swift and graceful, her body a slim knife slicing hot through soft butter. The water was hungry for her; it swallowed her eagerly into its depth. She was hungry for silence. She didn't struggle. Hallelujah's body bolted upright in her bed, yet she was not awake as you might imagine. Her eyes had rolled inside her head so only their white showed through the narrow slits of her barely parted eyelids. She'd stumbled to the kitchen. Her body knew the way and opened the refrigerator. She'd sat on the cold wood floor, awash in the stark white of the refrigerator light, and sunk her fingers into the chicken broth, gelatinized from the cold refrigerator air. Her hands found cooked chicken thighs. She brought one to her mouth. She ate it. She ate three more plump pieces of cold chicken and chewed at the gristle. She ate handfuls of fruit cake, she vomited chunks of barely chewed food, and she dug out sticky globs of blueberry pie and pushed it into her mouth. She tore open the plastic film covering a hunk of roasted ham, lifted the mound to her face and took giant bites, swallowing without chewing, the whole while whimpering between mouthfuls, "I'm sorry, I'll swim, let's swim, I'm sorry."

They stayed in Nova Scotia for weeks longer than planned, waiting in vain for Genevieve to turn up. Her parents had the local police searching for her. They tried to convince Elsewhere Patrice to leave his daughter with them, but his response of "Over my dead body" contained more venom than his daughter had ever witnessed from him.

In the taxi, on the way to Patrice's flat in the assisted living residence building on the Dartmouth waterfront, Hallelujah's grip on Patrice's hand tightens.

"T'as l'air stressé," he says.

"T'inquiète pas, Papa, je vais bien."

•

HALLELUJAH HAS JUST HAILED a taxi to head back to Blanca when she receives a text from Tafa:

It was boring without you, came home.
Tipsy (and horny).
Come here.

Soon, Hallelujah is at the flat again, a mirror of the place she has just moved into. The living-room lights are on, and except for Tafa's brown leather loafers strewn across the floor, things are as they left it only hours earlier. The tear is still there, smaller than Hallelujah had left it. It appears to be slowly sewing itself shut. She registers this with a small sense of urgency that quickens her pulse. She should go back, she should go back, but there's something ...

She looks through the box of framed photographs and sees that her Elsewhere self is darker and leaner, as though she spends more time in the sun. (She does. She works outside, sometimes in the sun, coordinating community gardens and greenhouses in food deserts throughout the province.) Hallelujah wants to drink every detail of the pictures, but there is no time.

In a dash, she is in the bedroom where Tafa is snoring under linen covers, their clothes in a crumpled pile at the side of the bed. Her other self keeps her journals in a green milk crate under the bed, just like her own self, except her container is a tan cardboard box. Still, like her, Elsewhere Hallelujah has each notebook labelled by year. Hallelujah selects 2002 and tucks it in the band of her stolen jumpsuit. Before she leaves the bedroom, she leans over Tafa and presses her face in the crook of their neck; she inhales deeply and plants a soft kiss on their cheek.

Her eyes are open now. So when she tugs the tear to fit herself through, she can see the fabric behind the air. As yet, there are no words to convey the colours, no adequate description for the absence of matter that envelops her. So for now, let's say ... luminous, radiating, bright, bright, sharp rays singing high-pitched bliss engulfing bliss, engulfing bliss. A hungry howl that swallows itself entirely, voracious. Bliss. Effervescent, kaleidoscopic. And the blackest ink, and the most open night sky expelling so many bursting suns, and the universes that exist momentarily on the skin of a soap bubble. And the colour of your energy when your heart is seized by your beloved, and the texture of your grandmother's prayers when she misses you—when she calls upon her god to guide you, and the taste of your very first inhale.

Hallelujah inhales sharp, sharp, to catch up to the breath that escapes her. She wonders if she will survive this magnificent unravelling, then she sees her other self and calms. They both calm when their eyes meet. She looks at her other self, at her freckled throat, and wonders if a stutter lives there too, if it coils itself around her tongue sometimes as well. Hallelujah smiles, and Hallelujah smiles simultaneously. They nod at each other, reach gingerly outstretched arms to touch, but an instant before their fingers meet, they are returned home.

3. *Here*

At home, Hallelujah sits on the floor of the apartment she shares with her lover, Tafa. She watches a peculiar tear in the air heal itself. She cannot tell you how long it takes, but she sits through the whole thing, stunned, silent. She marvels at the seam of golden light that patches the flaps of translucence that came apart as she squeezed through. She closes her eyes to imagine her other self on the opposite side of the sealing plane, then her eyes fly open when she feels something hit her cheek. She looks around to find a crumpled wad of paper. She smooths it to read her own sloppy handwriting, a message written in haste and thrown through the closing tear in the air.

It's not your fault.

You deserve to be spoiled rotten with good love. Believe it.

The tenderness of the message steals her breath again. She hiccups and sobs and watches the tear in the air close entirely.

•

TAFA STIRS HALF-AWAKE WHEN Hallelujah climbs into bed beside her. It's almost dawn, and the night knows. It begins its reluctant fade and slowly slinks into the light. Hallelujah buries her face in the crook of Tafa's neck and exhales.

Tafa, who smells of sweat and stale beer, mumbles, her words heavy with sleep, "You're you again."

"I am?"

"Mm-hmm."

Hallelujah wants to know how the night went. She wants to know everything, but she'll have to wait until morning. Then, she'll have to figure out what and how much to give away.

"Go back to sleep, love," she says, tangling her legs with Tafa's.

"Goose night, baby," Tafa lisps.

Hallelujah giggles softly and replies, "Goose night, Tafa."

But Tafa is already snoring again.

PLAYING DEAD

Trynne Delaney

BEFORE I ARRIVE, I must cross two thresholds. The first is a gate. As I approach, a sparrow flies silently above me. It's indistinguishable from any sparrow with a beating heart, except for its silence. Silence is such a luxury—the sound of surveillance. The metal plate slides open to let me through to a tunnel of green.

Despite the circumstances I've vacated and because of those you inhabit, we meet for the first time on the second threshold, this desolate obsidian stoop. The black stone beneath us captures the early summer heat, and like any valuable resource, you can't help catching it in your palm, can't help but to bring your golden palm to your chest, where your fingers spread into rays and your chest reaches through cotton to meet it. Your other hand reaches in my direction. Our palms touch. I let you fold my hand into yours. There is a sense that you're searching for familiarity between my cells. You close your eyes as you root around, which allows me to look over your face, where I conduct my own search across the craterless landscape of your skin. You could be my age. There's really no way to tell that you were born less than a year after my father.

It's only after I make the easy step across this second threshold into your home that you say the line I was told you would lead with: "Your father raised me," and the rest, "He brought me outside from where I was doing mathematics to try and save everyone." You shake your head at the trivial footnote of your youth. Of course, by every account it wasn't outside but your mathematics that saved everyone, which is to say all of us who lived outside, while you reside here: enclosed and clean.

You're someone my father hoped I'd never grow into, with my own tendency to stay indoors scribbling dreams of another world where there was nothing written. The threat of malignancy always seemed to rest at the edge of my voice, which he inspected and corrected. As he told it, he'd already raised you once and been disappointed; it could not happen again.

Reading through the lines of his history, I believe you loved him enough to save him, and now to save me, a refraction of him, that called up begging with a smile and an offer of service. You surrendered to my plea with grace. You said, "It's been hard since she left"—meaning: you didn't know what to do with your kids and you could afford to pay me somewhere between a pittance and everything to raise them before I got swallowed into the future with all the rest of outside. "For old times' sake."

What a tiny sentimentality. With all this power you are God and I am lucky.

•

"INTRODUCE YOURSELF. TELL THEM where you're from."

I soften my face into innocence. I say my name. I say, "I'm from here. Just like your father," and the children come into focus. There are two of them standing there, backlit in front of the floor-to-ceiling window: perfectly proportioned, sweet things, with halos of shiny dark hair and glowing skin. The way you look between them is how I've seen people look at kids on the bus when they're throwing a fit, somewhere between distant sympathy and disguised revulsion. Maybe I'm wrong. I'm not always the best at distinguishing between others' emotions and my own.

You introduce them—Rex and Bunny—then call them the opposite when they begin to race around the plush furniture, then scramble over it, one in pursuit of the other, their tiny fingers reaching into the couch's larval folds. Everything that could shatter shatters: vases, the transparent glass monitor that must be your television, the minimalist frames that contain white cellular structures embossed on rough white cardstock. The destruction happens faster than I can follow. With the habit of routine or performance, they wrestle in circles until I cannot tell where one ends and the other begins, whether the elder or younger is taller, whether these names are the ones I should call them. I am not sure I can tell them apart. I am not sure that you can even tell them apart.

Like a crack of thunder, your hands meet and they are still. "Quiet time," you say, "but first, shake your nanny's hand." The children do their best impression of their father's handshake. Then they return to their rooms to go about their secret business.

Nanny is a funny word. Where we come from we use it to refer to our grandmothers. The language you speak in this house has the same words but is not mine.

You shrug at the shards of glass and wires that cover the floor like the mythical ice fields, as if there's nothing you can do. A vacuum emerges from the wall and sucks the detritus up.

"It will all be recycled into new products." You pull a breath into your core, hold it, then let it go. The vacuum retreats and a mineral blue streak remains on the shining floor, a souvenir of the wreckage. "The manual help comes in on Tuesdays. She'll clean it up then." I nod in agreement and follow you wherever you're paying me to go next.

•

"IF YOU CAN'T AFFORD to be an artist, you can't afford to have morals when you need money." My mother told me this when I was offered the job and leaked despondent hot tears. The contract was too long a sentence. I couldn't speak aloud.

In her day she had done well dancing until her feet stopped and she became sullen. Her body ached constantly. I would bathe her in the evenings and we would hope and pretend that I was her mother and not the other way around. You would have found this position grotesque, I know it, standing over your own mother with a sponge while her bony hands held on to the edges of that yellowing tub as she laughed and laughed at something you'd both nearly forgotten, something only we knew and understood because of the world we inhabited and our place in it.

•

AFTER A LUNCH OF boiled eggs and broccoli you invite me into your office. I hesitate before stepping into what you describe as your most sacred space. The air inside is colder, and the sheer curtains are drawn so the cold overhead lighting dominates. "Better for brain function." You step onto your StairMaster. You gesture toward the window, so I walk to its edge. Like the windows in the living room, it spans from floor to ceiling and wall to wall. Although it is filtered for sunlight so I can't see everything in its true contrast, the window looks out onto the surprisingly wild back of the property where a wide and sparkling greenhouse sits nested in the field. "All the food we eat comes from there."

I hum as if impressed. I've heard that the soil here was cleansed when you bought the property. It's not like the soil at home. No mystery diseases propagating in its pores. "Not cleansing the soil would have been a sin," you tell me.

"Which?"

"A bit of all seven."

I turn my back to you and face the wall. I've seen where the runoff collects in the watershed just a thirty-minute walk from my mother's home. Lunch is not sitting well in my stomach. It's growing large, full of gas.

On the wall I now face is a sequence of three extremely muscular men. They flex their muscles and bare their teeth. Their oil-covered skin enhances the architecture of their bodies. Natural yet intentional—entirely produced, sculpted to signal … what? Control or commitment? Like yours, their bodies were the ultimate canvases. They're beautiful. How much our world has changed.

Certainly you are more muscular than these men. In the documentary on your life you said that you could lift anything in the house and maybe some of the decorative boulders that interrupt the back of the property. Your clothes must be tailored to accommodate your bulk. Unlike the men on your walls, what you do is not art. I'm almost sure of it. That's what you've called it at certain points, but your practice lacks a certain wonder. Something about the desperation that comes with the pursuit of immortality, the invisible resources that must churn and churn to keep the product of you fresh … what would one call that?

•

BUNNY RUNS AHEAD OF Rex into the field. Or Rex runs ahead of Bunny? Either way, their laughter rises high and bright above the maiden grass's feathery inflorescence. I lean against a grey boulder and take a sip of distilled water. One of the children's heads bobs above the grass momentarily. Wind rustles through the field, creating waves just like the ones I looked out onto only yesterday. The kids are jumping up and down, their heads coming in and out of view like buoys in the beige and green. One of them throws up their hands and screams so loud and hard that my heart races. It's as if they're drowning in the field. Their noise, so piercing and useless, reverberates. If they were in the ocean, by the time I got to them it would be too late.

When they run out of the field again, I wave them over. They come when they're called—well-trained little lap dogs. So far, they have not spoken in my presence unless spoken to or if they need to use the bathroom. I'm not sure if they're shy or polite. I ask what they saw in the field to try to understand what I think was good humour beneath all their shrieks.

Without acknowledging my question, they walk past me, inside. I follow them and make their scheduled snack: a grilled cheese that as far as I can tell does not contain actual cheese or bread and is lightly toasted, not grilled. Too much colour might signal disease. I've been warned.

•

THE CHILDREN ARE USED to the blood draws. I complete the first round on my third day as their nanny. They do not wince as I slip the needle under the fold of their elbows into their river-blue veins. The small silicone bags fill in my palm, hot, almost beating still. And then I hand them each a juice box that they suck dry before returning to tumbling around the house like violent dust bunnies.

I wasn't aware I would be responsible for this. Are they aware that you use their blood for your treatments? All of this is illegal, which means nothing in a different way to you than it does to me. Luxury is made of exemptions. I take such good care of the children and they're always making new blood. Are they aware? It's a renewable resource. You're not a vampire. They have a good life.

Are they aware? Of course. I didn't mean to suggest they weren't. Only that I wonder how they feel because I have the sense that when I approach them, they play dead with their feelings. I suspect that I'm the vampire for wanting to know them so that I can care for them better. That essentially, I might not be aware—that I might be exploiting them too. I want them to touch me, to climb on my back, to ask their father a question and have him look to me, then decide in looking to answer honestly.

•

AND ME, WHAT DID I learn from my father? A masculinity in gentleness that goes unnoticed. My own fingers' tremble as they gutted and deboned a mackerel. Fishing was the one thing he'd learned from his biological father, back when the border was still open and he'd gone down south to visit. It's a masculinity that is easy to hide here, soft as I am in an environment so hard. I can reshape myself easily when surveilled; I must, because what you want is a mother for your children that you do not have to see as an equal with desires.

I looked her up. I look just like her. It's funny. In the documentary they said she'd returned to her homeland somewhere between the weeds of the Sargasso Sea. They would not speak the name of her country because of how free it was. What a violence it was to say: returned. The documentary was made only three years before the borders closed for good. Do you remember her face? Did you expect to see her in me? There are no pictures here. All the walls are clean of history.

•

THE CHILDREN LET ME tuck them into their stiff linen sheets. They listen as I read the story they choose. It's a part of the evening routine that I'm surprised hasn't been automated. The small voice that comes from the steel box in the corner might've recited a children's story in a tone perfectly adjusted to make their heads nod and lips part for drool to seep into their pillows. This is the one thing they ask me for: they want me to read to them.

And so I read. I inject excitement into moments of tension and pull out funny voices to keep them engaged. Still, if they were having any reaction, I could not see it. They watch me with their sharp grey-brown eyes, silent and motionless. When I was a child, I had two little dolls that I'd set out in front of a desk where I'd play school. They were like these dolls. If I wanted to understand my effect on them, I had to extrapolate. As I finish the story, I realize my head is hot with embarrassment—I'm too old to play with dolls. I'm not sure I nailed the performance. Cold sweat leaks from my armpits.

They turn their faces away from me and close their eyes. "Goodnight," I whisper, and dim the light with a stroke of my fingertip on the nightstand. They do not rustle. When I leave their room and walk down the hallway, I do not hear the padding of bare feet or suggestions of play. I do not have to go back to tell them to go to bed and stop messing around. They've convinced me that they are asleep.

•

NO ONE HAS SHOWN me where to sleep and I have not found my bedroom. During the children's bedtime routine, you retire too, and I haven't found the proper moment during the day to ask you where I should sleep. The couch in the living room has worked as a place to sleep so far, but I have no blanket and the house cools down at night to optimize rest. Tonight, I consider knocking on your door. I know where you sleep, I see the red light glow from beneath your doorway. The hum of some machine penetrates the walls. A mist settles over me as the humidifying system engages to keep the house at forty-six percent humidity. The scent of ozone, creatine, and fresh sweat leaks from beneath your doorway. I bring my face closer to the crack. Folded almost in two, your musk grows stronger. My hand is raised, but I cannot bring myself to interrupt your sleep—I suspect you would not respond kindly to the interruption, given the time you spend reviewing your biometrics each morning.

Besides, I don't know if you'd hear me if I did knock. Surely you wear earplugs or use some other form of sound therapy to align your brainwaves for an optimized sleep.

My own heart is restless, and I don't know if I'll be able to sleep. A throbbing has reached from my toes, up past my thighs, and begun to settle there. I let my feet lead me out the back door and into my shoes. Your house is not lit past 9:00 p.m.—all lights are out. I let my feet lead me back toward the field where the children were playing. What did they see? Behind me the house grows small; its corners reflect in the moonlight, then bend and begin to disappear. Inside the field my vision is shuttered, grass brushes my arms, raises hairs then skin in goosebumps. I am walking downhill into a kind of shallow valley. I am walking away from you more and more urgently. Deeper into the field and farther from wherever my bed is. The flame of acid reflux licks within my chest, my heart might seize, and my legs are burning, I've cut myself, hot blood runs down my cheek. The sharp of dried grass imprints my knees among the rustling and low purring of sparrows who rest in the field. My fingers slip into my pants, and in the bosom of the valley I see myself as if mirrored clearly for the first time since I've arrived. I see myself, an apparition, a few steps in front of me, their head back, wailing in pleasure. No one will hear and no one will see what I am except me.

•

ONE WHALE WASHED UP onto the beach, and then more. The rot of them was so thick on the air no one could sleep. Every night, everyone in the town you and my father grew up in would go out and try to break down the bodies. You were on the disintegration crew. There's a picture of you in biohazard gear with what I think is the posture of a smile on your shoulders. That first whale, I could not understand its vastness, let alone the others'. For their bodies to cover the beach, which curved around the edge of the earth—the sheer amount of information, you said, massaging your feet. You had to cut it into smaller pieces. You had to burn it all to ash.

I wake on the porch, in front of the doorway. You are facing me, about a metre away with your asshole high, stretched toward the sun. "Vitamin D." You pull your cheeks apart. You hold my gaze. It's sunrise, which is when my work officially begins.

Rex and Bunny appear from inside and kiss you on each glowing cheek in tandem. You squelch kisses to the air like they can touch your children. They come over to me and grip my hands, help me rise to make their breakfast.

We eat. It's yesterday all over again: the tumbling, their screeching in the field. This is what life will be for you, forever, if you are successful. You excuse yourself as the team of doctors arrive, showing off the new side effects of youth. They deliver your stats on the living room's glass screen, one by one, dryly. I do not know if those numbers mean anything to you. I dole out snacks and scrape the insides of the children's mouths with cotton swabs, then swirl the cotton swabs in liquid. Before supper, we walk down the path to the gate to slip the packages containing what you described as their essences into the clamped arms of a drone.

•

WHEN I DO RECEIVE the money it's more than enough. This has never happened before. Where I come from (here) it doesn't happen unless you cut down all the trees and renounce disease despite its slow creep into you and your loved ones' lives. I send half of the money back home with love and certainty that my head will remain above water. For now. The money talks. The money asks me to stay.

I say yes. For now. I watch as they inject your skin with organic compounds and massage blisters away. How much does that cost? If I knew, would it make me want more? I want to ask the slight woman who presses the end of the needle so deep and fast without making you wince: *How much?* But even she might not know. Maybe none of us could imagine. It's something that might stretch beyond us. Something you may repeat to your staff in your lonely certain future, long after I'm dead and gone.

MOTHER, FATHER, BABY

Lue Palmer

ABI-GAYE'S APARTMENT WAS RUFFLED and out of place, her things pushed aside to make room for her mother's belongings. Her mother was a proud woman and she framed her life in photographs: a portrait of her siblings and parents, her wedding photo, each of her children's graduation and school pictures, with their hair pasted to politeness. The newly mounted photographs pressed themselves against the walls and glared outward; their tight smiles breathed through their teeth, and necks strained against collared uniforms.

She had set her husband's deep-blue urn on the whatnot in the corner, and from his roost Abi-gaye's father surveyed the kitchen. He sat comfortably beside a large wooden clock that looked down impartially on the apartment.

When she was little, Abi-gaye had awoken to the

sound of its unbothered ticking. Her eyes opened in the dark, the shadows flitting irritably around her room. She pulled herself from the bed and followed the kitchen light down the hallway. She moved quietly, afraid she would be punished for being out of her room at night.

Her father sat in shadow at the kitchen table. At first Abi-gaye thought he must be asleep, with his tall frame resting on his arms. But then he looked up. His eyes playful, he pressed a finger to his lips and gestured to Abi-gaye to come close. In front of him sat a can of condensed milk, opened with two slits on either side, enough to let out a long stream of thick, sweet syrup. He turned the can over and let the milk coil.

"Sit down, baby," he whispered. Abi-gaye watched the milk pool on the spoon.

•

"YOU HOME THEN, BABY?" Her mother padded into the dining room, her tall figure bent low.

"Yes, mummy." Abi-gaye had walked the distance from work across the dry grass courtyard, surrounded by midrises on all sides. Her head ached with the heat.

Abi-gaye turned to her mother and looked her up and down. She had taken to wearing church clothes, at all times dressed for worship as if she were in constant need of forgiveness. She wore a long blue button-down dress, neatly pressed, and a wide-brimmed hat. Abi-gaye's mother fussed with her starched-straight clothing and looked at her daughter.

"I've been out visiting Merle and her little grandbaby," she said, twisting her lips. "That child is always telling lies." Her mother paused to consider her daughter, looking over her heavy eyes and full figure.

"I told her she ought to wash the girl's mouth out." Abi-gaye clutched the table edge under her mother's gaze.

•

THE SHADOWS HAD BEEN restless in Abi-gaye's childhood room, and she often stayed up with them at night as they played across the windows and tumbled over the floor. At times, the shadows became rude and misbehaved, looming above Abi-gaye as she hid under the covers, tugging at her hair.

In the evening as her mother slept in the spare room, Abi-gaye scrubbed the apartment, coating the kitchen in bleach. She wiped around her father's blue urn, where it stood a head above the kitchen and looked down on her. She opened the windows and let the fresh air come through. She powdered bleach in the sink to soak. She breathed in deeply and it smelled harsh and fresh.

Abi-gaye put herself to bed. She slid underneath the sheets and tucked herself in. She breathed in the warm air. She lay awake, and the hours of nighttime tiptoed toward each other. Abi-gaye felt a shadow lean close and linger at her ear. She swatted at it and clamped her eyes shut. They kept at it until she was angry for sleep. Abi-gaye sat up in bed, looking out of the window at the buildings around her for a source of disturbance on the night air. Her eyes made rounds of the room, squinting closely at the shadows hiding in the dresser and hanging between the scarves on the door.

She buried her head beneath her arms and willed herself to get drowsy. On the edge of sleep, she heard a baby cry out in the darkness, the sound rolling deep from the child's throat.

•

ABI-GAYE PASSED HERSELF IN the hallway, a portrait of a girl pinned against a wall. Her eyes wide and mouth slightly open. Her school uniform had been pressed neatly for the picture. A bitter taste had stuck to her lips where her mother had scrubbed her mouth. Her round belly and small breasts were hidden shamefully behind the frame of the photograph.

Her mother was in the living room, tall in a blue buttoned coat and church hat, readying herself for service. She had always worn this outfit to match her husband's Sunday blue tie, which drooped downward whenever he leaned low to arrange his family in the church pew, where they sat in erect and attentive lines. Her mother sat beside her father, with one eye on their children and one eye on the service—her hands constricted in gloves too tight, her nails grating against the cotton.

Abi-gaye sat directly between her parents and younger brothers, who slid their bottoms back and forth on the wooden pews, dropped off the benches and stared underneath them, looked upside down at nylon ankles and the backs of hanging skirts. Until they were abruptly yanked by their collars to their seats, and sat the rest of service with their hands under their bottoms and their faces blank, rubbing sore necks. And at the end of service, her father led them in grasping the hands of the pastor and the church families, insisting on reaching each of them and wishing them all blessings.

Her mother left for church quietly this afternoon, carrying her sins heavily in a large square clutch.

"Goodbye, baby," she told Abi-gaye, and then blew a kiss to her husband's ashes, sleeping soundly in the pot.

Alone, Abi-gaye laid her body down again, the heat of the afternoon coaxing her into an unforgiving sleep. She awoke in a sweat in the early evening, head heavy and full of sound—a baby crying, its voice drawn into a taut string that threatened to snap.

Abi-gaye's breath came quick as she rose and searched the windows outside. The evening was undisturbed except for the yellow light that lay across the dry grass. Abi-gaye dashed for the door, flung it open, and walked heavily down the hallway, her bare feet beating on the floor. She stepped out into the open courtyard and looked up at the buildings around her, making a square of the sky, but saw nothing but the nighttime, a few open windows with lights on. Still she could hear the baby's cries mixed with the cool singing of the night air and the heat pressed against her chest, between her legs, and under her arms.

Away across the yard, a woman walked tall in a blue coat and wide church hat. The long sweep of her thin body standing out against the shadow, she clasped a child by the hand. The baby raised her head. Her heavy eyes seemed to call out in the dark. Abi-gaye tilted an ear across the yard. The child opened its mouth and spoke:

Mi must tell she "pickney nuh say nuh lie."
Mi bring her dark and mek her cry.
Yuh must tell he "pickney no wan fi play."
Soon he come, soon dash away!

The tall woman clasped the baby's hand tightly, her eyes hidden behind the hat. One foot and then another, the child led her away into the shadows.

Abi-gaye stood alone in the courtyard, her mouth gone dry. She stared after them until she could see nothing. The darkness pressed in on her and the sky breathed down kindly. The nighttime came and wrapped itself around her legs and under her arms. Shadow and light cupped the back of her neck and wove into her hair, came dripping down her calves and clutched her feet. They carried and walked her body that way, across the dry grass. They walked her through the doors and down the hallway. They laid her gently across the bed. Then the shadows curled up softly on her belly and fell asleep.

Abi-gaye awoke fresh and afraid. Her eyes opened to the blanket of night, the shadows resting humbly around her room. She left them breathing smoothly like nighttime babes. She pulled herself from the bed, followed a beam of light down the hallway into the cool kitchen. She moved quietly, the brown clock ticking out its heavy rhythm, sweat pooling on her lip. The kitchen was silent and nearly empty; the deep-blue urn sat partially concealed in shadow. It seemed to gesture her closer. Abi-gaye reached for him, pulled down the handsome blue pot from where it surveyed the kitchen. She breathed deeply into her body, filling her lungs up, and opened the top.

Abi-gaye peered inside at the grey ashes. She let her breath out and watched the dust inside catch it and reach up to meet the air. She watched her father fill up her kitchen. She watched him settle on the counters, on the table, and across the floor.

Abi-gaye held the blue pot between her hands, and her father smiled out of the dark, his beard and teeth coated with sweet milk. His breath smelled so close it turned her stomach.

"Come here, baby," he said. Abi-gaye stopped breathing. Her legs dangled from her seat and swung in the air. She shrunk down, smaller and smaller, her arms shaking from her shoulders down to her fingers. The pot felt bigger in her small hands, so heavy on her lap, it crushed her legs and pinned her there.

Her father came closer to her until his lips rested next to her ear and his hands held her small face. He breathed in deeply, inhaling the words from her belly into his mouth until she could not speak. She screamed, but made no sound. Only her eyes went wide as her father lingered, pressed close to her and smelling of sweetness.

Abi-gaye searched the room and found a woman's face in the brown clock glass, her heavy eyes frantic.

She felt the woman's hands reach down over her own, clasp them strong and brace her arms.

The baby and the woman lifted the blue pot from her lap and pushed it away across the room. It hit the sink edge and cracked. The dust spread in a cloud. Her father lay in shards on the ground, blood leaking like ink out of his body. So much blood it spread across the floor and crept between her toes, soaking the underside of her feet. She stood up and watched him choking on the air, growing still and quiet, smaller and smaller.

Abi-gaye reached under the sink and powdered the bleach on the floor. She squatted and rubbed it in.

DEH AH MARKET

Whitney French

> *Where an estate had land not wanted for cane, the slaves were usually allowed to cultivate food crops on it in their spare time ... which they often had to do at night. These foods and materials were raised primarily for their own use ... surpluses came to be taken to local markets and exchanged for other commodities or sold for cash.*
> —Sidney Mintz, "Provision Grounds,"
> *from* The Jamaica Reader

IT'S RISKY BUT THERE'S no other way. It'd be impossible to taga-taga a coal stove on the TTC, so Aunty makes a deal with the man who runs the convenience store. She pays him to keep the small aluminum charcoal cooktop and the bags of Kingsford coals (in a pinch, she'll get by with the Royal Oak brand) and send Cousin, her nephew, to carry it to market. These people don't like open-flame cooking but she has to risk it. Roasted breadfruit is her bestseller.

When Cousin nods to the man who runs the convenience store, an uncle-figure from Ethiopia who's watched businesses come and go against the clatter of the Metrolinx's decade-long construction, he nods back. And in a few moments a heavy coal stove, discoloured and blackened from use is in their hands. The walk isn't far, less than three blocks, but eventually Cousin's forearms begin to strain. That's because they are caught in a loop again. Second time this week. And the body knows how long they've been holding the coal stove, how time is transmuted between the Just Incredible Hair salon and the More Than a Hair Cut barbershop. Cousin walks the same block twenty-eleven times over, each time pushing their thick locs out of their face. Tries tippy-toeing to the northside of the street, then back to the south. No use.

Cousin slips. Not onto the ground but slips out. Slips away from the man who owns the convenience store, who shouts, "Where you come from?" when they emerge from the blue-grey basement door. Slips past cramped housing buildings across the street from other housing buildings. Slips. Their mom used to live on Eglinton Avenue West when she was their age, but she's back in Jamaica now. It's a comfort, perhaps, to know that even if this farmer's market didn't exist when she lived here, the street certainly did. Their mom walked Eg Ave, maybe even walked by Hot Pot Restaurant and smelled the jerk chicken grilling in the repurposed oil-barrel-turned-barbeque. Maybe she jaywalked to the south side of the block from the north side, between whizzing traffic merging off the Allen. Maybe she bought coco bread from Spence's Bakery like they did, like they often did, to tide them over before helping Aunty at the market. They think about that sometimes. A V of sweat darkens the front of their polyester shirt.

Most times though, Cousin knows better. Specifically on a day like today when Papa Baker announced for the third time to stop troubling him about no Jamaica. "We don't have it this year." A child gets weary after not seeing their mother for three years. Can't blame Cousin for begging their legal guardian, even if it means being showered in a hailstorm of anger. Gotta try, nuh. There was more than a whisper of hope, what with a vague mention of packing up a barrel. But the man's tone was clear.

Cousin tries to slip out of the loop, walks back into the rhythm of the man-who-owns-the-convenience-store's nod, but the glitch repeats the nodding motion. Cousin jaywalks into the Droste effect of windows from community housing buildings: mirroring an infinity; loops back as the jerk pan opens and closes and then, as the smoke plumes out from it, reversing back into the smoker pipe; loops alongside the watery sheen of back-trunk june plums that change ever so slightly each time Cousin sees them (and now they too crave june plum on their tongue).

Cousin finally escapes the loop, past the bustling entrance. An eyeblink of déjà vu and they've returned to linear. There's a shiver down their spine, despite it being thirty degrees Celsius. They went someplace else, and maybe this time, they *when* someplace too.

Low level clouds skim the top of Cousin's locs. When Cousin glances upward, the clouds scramble feverishly to the rim of the sky, a little shy about playing so close to humans head tops.

Meanwhile, the coal stove, compact, durable, is delicately placed near Aunty's feet. Instant relief from Cousin followed by cut-eye from Aunty. She's annoyed for Cousin's tardy, dismisses them. Her straw baskets dazzle people with produce many haven't seen since their childhood, and the smell of roasted breadfruit is her ultimate lure.

"Nothing like Spanish Town Market," Aunty reminds Cousin, but it's the only market they know: a crowded parking lot full of Trinidadians, Bajans, Haitians, East Africans, Chinese Canadians, and even one or two white vendors selling not so much produce but products: homemade hot sauces, vegetarian and vegan patties, organic multigrain bread, sorrel (so much sorrel), shea butter, soy-based candles, fair-trade Ethiopian coffee, pepper-infused honey, and other novelty items. The Afro-Caribbean Farmers' Market is only into its third year, but its popularity brings liveliness to an otherwise construction-choked Eglinton block.

Aunty is one of the few folks who sells Caribbean produce. Other vendors wave and blow with the breeze, but Aunty is stone. When Cousin arrives with the coal stove, she's surrounded by a mountain of breadfruit sitting on a lawn chair, the Canadian Tire logo faded from use. There are small bundles of callaloo, and quarts of peppers nestled in green reusable cartons arranged neat on the table where the two squeeze up next to each other.

"What me need sign fuh?"

The grill shakes and bounces against the weight of the breadfruit, sphere-green at first, but the fire sears away at the skin leaving it transformed, shrivelled and ashen. Watching her hands turn over the breadfruit, Cousin thinks of basketball, admires Aunty's skilled handling as she almost dribbles the ball in fire. But quickly the allure wanes and the heat swells—mid-August humid neck-stick-heat overwhelms. All the sides of the fruit are charred and cooled. The air bends and ripples against the heat. Cousin regrets spending their Sunday so close to black tarmac—the air bends and ripples against the heat—that is until Aunty says, "Never have chil'ren of my own to bring ah market." Then they feel shitty.

Cousin's turn now. Silently, they peel back the charred skin with a knife hidden in the folds of tablecloth and puncture the deformed globe just so, applying pressure between blackened skin and buttery flesh. Aunty teases how they stay ropey and lean, tallawah but Cousin knows that just means they have stamina for monotonous tasks. Soon Cousin cubes the breadfruit and stabs a toothpick into each peg, dusts salt, and places the food on a platter lined in tinfoil. Samples: Aunty's oldest trick.

The clouds plunge lower once more, as if they decided

all on their own, up there in the sky above, a new way of breathing.

"See them clouds?" she gestures, hours later as the crowd dies down. Cousin nods. A crack of thunder underscores her proclamation.

•◉•

IF YOU CATCH MS. YVETTE in the market in a good mood—her default: raspy baritone champions over all others down the stretch leading to the covered area, "Pumpkin two-fifty!" with interjections of "Hello, miss, a dat mi frock?" and you too can witness her seamless sell-plus-compliment combo—then you know that you'll have a good day and no badmindedness will follow you. But if you catch Ms. Yvette in a not-so-good mood—her skilled finesse no match for "Eh, business *slow*," and fresh food spoil quick and the wrinkle in her forehead creases as she calculates losses (today there will be losses)—then it's a different type of day. Before noon, when her flimsy hat is no defence against the vigilant tropic and a cartman clips Ms. Yvette's toes not once but twice since morning … when invisible creatures knock off the coconut from the bottom of the pile, a hollow rhythm from a fruit avalanche echoes along the path leading down the stretch near the meat shop, then you'll hear, "Pumpkin t'ree-hundred!"

Today is a not-so-good day. The duct tape that held the tarpaulin together for months, it decides today … today!

to lose its stick after last night's moist air (but no rain) and expose the triangular-cut tear right above Ms. Yvette's stall, anointing her head with a beam of light, hot and merciless, kissing her forehead. Her hands are callused orators of their own accord. They cradle coin and fasten her hair curlers; wipe babies bottoms and carry crates of carrot, ginger, yam, and dasheen; grip machete to slice jelly with wrist-precision, but fumble when it comes to texting her son in England on WhatsApp. Those hands are awnings from the aggressive sun. The wind blows the tarpaulin another twist and the sun catches her once again, sideways. An awful dance across her skin. "They playing with me today," she whispers. "And that gyal late again."

•◉•

WELLINGTON STREET
    Cumberland Road
    Old Market Street
    —all at her back.

Cuz flits and veers toward the Spanish Town Market (on haste!) as old-school dancehall fades in and out of earshot. She dodges past the bar with the hand-painted scriptures scrawled across the entrance while the soccer game blares, clashing with the music. Men in their thin off-white tanks and threadbare jerseys re-enact the last play, feet swinging, arms clambering over tables, drinks, voices colliding. Cuz hops across the gully gratings that smell of sewage, her own small frame unnoticed by the bustle of the street. She walks double-time at the same speed of the taxi pile-up, marketgoers hailing down a ride to get out of the heat before noon. Soon, behind a crumbling brick wall before the opening of the Spanish Town Market, she cotches herself near a dilapidated old as sin building—the old firehall or maybe old archives library or maybe old public washroom—and squats at the foot of the door. There's no knob and the paint peel is an ashy colour related to grey and blue.

Stillness. Cuz parses out the sounds of the city and swallows up the noise with her steady breath. Her sandalled feet ache, and Cuz folds herself into the corner of the doorframe like a hidden spider. *Rap, rap, rap!* Three knocks—sharp but undistinguished amongst the bustle, no one notices her banging. But she wasn't knocking for someone who lives in Dela Vega.

A pause ...

... on the dancehall music, on the soccer enthusiasts and taxi horns. On the higgler's arcade of women's clothing across the way—hangers holding printed skirts hand-stretched into circles for shapely women, sports caps, and "No Problem Man" low-quality tees, all the clothes hanging from the grill caught in the tropic air—frozen. Cuz shifts in her seat, the only person, the only anything on the entire block, moving.

Rap, rap, rap! Three punctuated knocks echo back, completing the call-and-response. The door squeals open to a peek into an overstocked Toronto-based convenience store's basement.

Behind the portal door, Cousin flashes a toothy smile. Side-by-side they doppelgänger each other with slight deviations: same face shape, different eye colour, same posture, different skin tone.

Soon the kin twins slap hands loud and pull into each other in a familiar embrace. On Cousin's side of the open door, the only indication that the world has stopped is an unmoving clock on the wall and a portable fan's streamers suspended mid-air.

"'Sup, Cuz?"

"Nothing. Bored."

"Me too."

Cousin raises their chin, glances over Cuz's shoulder to capture as much of the scene behind her as possible. Cuz's face quips wordlessly, "Whatchu looking for?" Or the better question, who? Cousin flings a stiff grin; it rises and falls from their face. As tempting as it was, who knows what crossing the threshold would do to their bodies?

Like an odd little routine, the two sit on either end of their respective doorways, legs sprawled out. She is spaghetti on the floor, all legs and limbs and limp. Cuz is finally getting used to how much Cousin mirrors her movements (or how she mirrors Cousin's?)—from the way they both rub their eyes, kiss their teeth, take up or don't take up space. Unlike her older brother, who is all heels and elbows and cuts away any room Cuz had to just be herself.

She sees how Cousin is aware of the ground beneath them in the same way she works alongside the air to run and move and dance.

"Yuh bring di sumthing?"

"Dun know. I mean ... yeah." Cousin gives Cuz Dollarama headphones in exchange for three june plums.

"Thanks."

"T'anks." As a reflection of the other, both cousins secure their gifts in opposite pockets.

"So how long should we keep doing this?"

"Doing what?

"You know," Cousin gestures exaggerated swooping circles between the doorframe. "Passing things through the portal."

"How you mean?"

"I dunno ..." Cousin thought about how if Cuz wanted to visit foreign and they wanted to see their mother, perhaps this was the best way to do it. But something visceral prevented them, and likely prevented Cuz too. Nothing is ever so easy; there's always something you give up as payment for quick passage.

"I dunno. Haven't you noticed things are different?"

"So? Don't mean we cause dem."

"True. I'm just saying ..."

"Ah wuh yuh a say?"

"Something feels off, I guess. The last few days." The time loop for one. "But you're right, it's nothing."

Cuz ignores them, distracted as she's prying her new

headset out of the packaging and finally plugging them into her phone, satisfied with her treasure.

"Yuh fret too much."

And it was at that moment the edges of the taxis and contours of the fan begin to quiver. They both jerk forward unconsciously, nose-to-nose, close enough to see the colour of the other's eye bleed into their own iris. A signal not to miss.

"We should head back."

"Uh huh. Otherwise it'll be nothing but Ms. Yvette's lip the whole taxi home."

They both giggle in eerie unison. And stop abruptly, disturbed.

"Okay, Cuz, say less. Easy eh?" Cousin stands to hug Cuz goodbye. They are exactly the same height. To the quarter inch.

"Later, Cousin."

They close the door, synchronized, and from either side where they stand, the air is sealed between the doorframe and hisses.

◉◎◉

MS. YVETTE WAS BORN a monozygotic twin and she likes to pepper conversations with, "Well, me and my twin sistah," and most people allow her to feel sensational for a few seconds with that piece of intrigue. Somewhere along the way, the twins lost their specialness, lost connection with one another, unthermalized and disentangled with little notice. Ms. Yvonne, who strictly goes by Vonnie now that she's back on the island, never tells people she's a twin. Doesn't tell people much at all. These days Yvette and Yvonne are more acquaintances than siblings, much less anything as fascinating as twins. And still, whenever Ms. Yvette sits down in the market to shell peas and pass the time, the muscle memory returns to her, like something a hitch-up in her body and glitch-up in her head. Ms. Yvette is taken back to the days when she and her twin sister were young-young and would sit in the grass, back-to-back racing to see who can shell the basket of gungo peas faster. "Done!" and Yvette would turn around to see if her sister was cheating, but ah true, like lightning, she done dem off. A few times they drew a tie, but Yvette never best her sister, not once. *Done!*

Not too many fascinating tidbits punctuate her life beyond that; her siblings, her twin and her older brother Baker, have scattered about, without paying her too much mind. Gladys' wash belly, a full seven minutes younger than Yvonne. And Lady Gladys, a mother tired of mothering, who was done with three kids when many her generation had all eight, nine, ten babies—that was an interesting woman, a woman who saw things. Understood the unexplainable that her church folk would shush away with a white-gloved wave. Gladys, a shapely, god-fearing woman, recognized the shadowed things that escaped God's purview and looked at these stranglings dead on. Square eyed. Beings who double-dutch between dimensions and rope in chaos and calamity from their world. So, by the time she pushed her last child into our world, a terribly ordinary girl, nothing left in time-space could frighten her. The possibilities that existed had already filled her eye, and she bore witness to the worst of it.

What Gladys knew, this brilliant, big woman—although she had to leave sixth form because of the hurricane and no one else was going to feed the babies—she knew about quantum. Shadows in the market, time swallowed by darkness. Time layered over present moments, time glitching and birthing oddities in the body clock. She knew that just like twins run in the family, cousin-twins run in the family too. Cousins born the same day from different mothers who are twin-kin. Two entangled particles moving and growing and living as an echo of the other, forever linked, forecasting and backcasting, special local relativity. How it go, because even though Yvette and Yvonne stopped talking to each other, they were riding the same wave of contractions when they birthed their own children, overlapping their pain in 4-1-1 timing across ocean. Gladys, who professed to feeling a storm in her bones and was always right, who knew her way around a portal, who in the end choked on a Bronshtein sugar cube and died in mere moments, she knew quantum very well. Every shadow that drapes itself across the market is an alternate possibility of any choice chosen and any choice not chosen. Like the parallel lives of cousin-twins. Particles love fuh ramp, no matter how far apart they are.

° ◎ °

UNLIKE COUSIN, CUZ DIDN'T slip into a time loop on their way to the marketplace, on their trek to Ms. Yvette, but she still reach late all the same. She hated being there, her lone and monotonous job of wrapping thyme and scallion into bundles while Ms. Yvette scream down the market 'bout how her pumpkin is best. Every so often, the older lady bats at Cuz's hands, undoes a few bundles and swipes at her again, scoffing, "Really. *Really?*" and Cuz would have to do it all over again. She waits for Ms. Yvette to go chat with her friend dem so Cuz can test out the full range of her new headphones (the bass' not bad!) and drown out the noise, sink into her music. She is never one for sitting still too long, even as a baby she'd get 'way, but with the earbuds she'd at least have a chance to phantom her new dance moves in her mind, rockaway in her headspace freely. Away from anyone else. Small solitudes.

She really thankful that Cousin is so willing to trade. Plus, it's a slow day; she just needs to collect from three-four people and can soon zone out the rest of the time.

A roar disrupts Cuz's meditation. She is halfway done with the thyme-scallion, but Ms. Yvette returns sooner than expected and plucks the earbud from Cuz's ear.

"Ouch!" Even though it don't hurt.

"You want something to bawl 'bout?" Cuz is immune to being cussed at, and Ms. Yvette isn't even all that mean most days. She knows Ms. Yvette will never bring down the full force of her anger on her ever; she's the dead-stamp of Gladys, and because she favours her mother's mother; because the ache of the matriarch's death still lingers in Ms. Yvette's walk full stop, no real punishment will come down on Cuz. Hereditary luck.

Under the layer of Ms. Yvette's tirade, she hears screams from a woman a few stalls over.

"How yuh mean drop on her suh?"

"Mi seh, a whole heap come down on har like WHOAH!"

"Ah dat fuh yuh problem, misses …"

"Foolishness."

"Uh-uh. Serious t'ing?"

"Is true! Snow mi see snow!"

"Stop yuh noise."

"S-N-O-W. Ah wah mi see, suh mi say!"

Even Ms. Yvette mid-cussing stops to glean into the commotion. She instructs Cuz to stay put as she leaves her post to find answers. When she returns, her anger from before is replaced with bewilderment.

"Poor woman sick now. Bad." Cuz pieces together a story of impossibility: a woman not even five stalls away is covered head to toe in white, powdery heavy-set snow that was gathering in the folds of the tarp above her. There is no snow anywhere else to be found according to Ms. May, who tells Ms. Rose who tells Ms. Yvette. The woman is chilled to the bone.

◎●◎

COUSIN WATCHES IN SILENCE how Aunty grips the front-room chair—a back home artifact—her fingers wrap around its arch, keeping her steady as she puts on shoes. These days, Cousin will quickly place Aunty's loafers on the seat so she won't have to bend so deep to collect them off the floor. The bare lightbulb that once haloed Aunty's head needs changing, but they've both been too busy to remember to replace it. Cousin isn't tall enough to reach, even with the stepladder. Papa Baker grunts when he flicks the switch on and off. He's been tricked. Again and again, as if he swore he lives in a house where people care about the state of the house (although he too never made any attempt to do much about the light). Best not to be home at all. Not in a house like that, not too long; and sometimes Cousin misses him, the way he says, "Laudgyad-eva," under his breath, but mainly Cousin relishes in being in Papa Baker's absence. In being okay with the late-summer sun, flooding the front walkway with long stretches of day. Aunty says, before Cousin was born, the Toronto Housing Commission wanted to move them to a smaller complex with a bedroom window facing a brick wall—and who knows what that'd do to her! Head tek was already getting ahead of her from time-to-time. Cousin's arrival meant a big fat check beside the [children] box of the application form, meant a window facing the southeast, meant bright mornings and slow movement toward fixing light bulbs in summer.

In the walkway, Cousin could hear the dingy sound of pop rap in their headset slung over their neck. Turning it down, rubbing their temple, they feel a throbbing. Both Aunty and Cousin felt it, the atmospheric pressure drop, tension migraines appearing almost out of nowhere. The sun-spilling window rumbles a caution. They said the forecast called for abnormally strong winds, don't?

Cousin and Aunty were too dizzy to clean the front entrance, although it's been a long time since it was tidied up: shoes mountain beside an empty rack, umbrellas sprouting from rain boots that should have been stored away seasons ago. Sandals with busted clasps and flip-flop soles splay open like crocodiles' mouths. Cousin's left sneaker sits amongst the rubble—weathered Jordan's scribbled with pitiful scuff marks—and they slip their feet in.

Cousin drops their shoe abruptly. A delicate shrill, the phantom-feel of something feathery and unexpected grazes their fingers. Instinctually they whisper, "Not roaches again." Maybe it's just ants this time. Flashback of last summer's scatterings and small agonies. Startled, Cousin imagines squashing whatever decided to take up residence in their left shoe. Blood rushes in their ears and the air chimes still.

No need to bend down and investigate as moments later an emerald-breasted doctor bird whizzes out the mouth of the shoe, its red sword tail whipping in the air like an after-image of small fireworks. The creature sports a cluster of feathers at the nape of its neck and a tuft of golden brown on its chest.

It takes a moment for Cousin's eyes to adjust to the disorienting speed of the doctor bird, with its small black head and its brown human eyes. Cousin knows that there were so few flowers on their block and the bird may very well die without pollen. Sugar water is a possibility, maybe leave some in an open bowl. But before Cousin can move to the kitchen, the doctor bird smashes its tiny body against the wall, over and over, frenzied and destructive, too fast for them to stop it. The bird collapses like pulp on the door mat.

◉◎◉

MYSTERIOUS NEW-GROWTH ACKEE TREES KILL LOCAL SQUIRRELS.

MARKET WOMAN FROM SPANISH TOWN PUMMELLED BY AVALANCHE OF SNOW.

COMMUTER CONFUSION AS ROADSIDE GOATS BLOCK PATH WALKWAY FOR HOURS.

HALFWAY TREE AN UNLIKELY SOURCE OF MAPLE SYRUP? MORE AT SIX!

◉◎◉

THE NEXT TIME COUSIN opens the doorway, Cuz isn't there. In fact, it's dark on the other side. Sweat gathers quickly round the front of Cousin's forehead. Heat blazes. The night air draws them in, tempting Cousin to cross the threshold into eventide. Mosquitos hover near the door; some whizz by the entrance, enchanted by the light, seduced by Cousin's blood-scent. Pungent and sweet. Yet the most overwhelming of sensations is the distinct slicing of machete tearing through bush.

"Who there?"

A shadow darts toward the door, a twinkle of moonlight catches the tip of a machete. *Slam!* Cousin closes the portal and grows space between their body and the door. Heartbeat in the throat. The regularity of the store basement droops long and misshaped against the extraordinariness of the world on the other side.

"I say, who's there?" a muffled voice through the door, a young woman determined to break it down. Cousin falters. *Run, nuh, run!* Scramble up the steps, forget this place, surrender to the vibrancy of the Sunday afternoon in your own time. Forget the sweeping intoxication.

Moments later, a gentle tapping. She's using the butt of the machete, in a child-game rhythm. Cousin doesn't trust it but is compelled to open the door all the same. They're in too deep.

Standing behind the open door, at precisely the same height as them, stands Hermana, a dark-skinned girl in an oversized Osnaburg frock and a wide-brimmed course hat. Her bleach-white headwrap peeks underneath. The air around her is electric in a way that reminds Cousin of Cuz. The artificial light from the basement fixture causes Hermana to squint a moment, otherwise, they both stare at each other's uncanny for a whole minute. Punctuated behind Hermana, the same chorus of chopping persists, cracking bush against cutlass, underscored by the odd squawk of an owl and the faint conversation of "just spread it like this, that's how crops need to grow." Lapses of long silences. Longer breezes. Eventually Hermana slices through the stillness.

"You's my cousin too?"

"Looks so."

Hermana cocks her head. She's a girl without a childhood. Her sun-weathered skin and faint scars age her. The world behind her is anything but empty, although Cousin cannot see beyond the black. Or they think they can, until a new sheet of dark covers the landscape before their eyes adjust. Hit with an unsourced knowing, Cousin realizes these are cane cutters' children. Young people who loath anything sweet on the tongue.

"When you from?"

"Uhhh?"

"*When* is you from? I from 1824."

"Oh. Oh!"

"That's what the other one said."

Cousin smiles, feeling a bit at ease that Cuz met this new person at a different when.

"Have you seen her? Like lately?"

"Well. I'm still learning how this works. We only get to night-farm every fortnight and some Sundays. S'been a while since the door open."

"Gotcha," was all that Cousin could manage. That could mean anything really, backtracking and foretracking, things are stretching into a new shape now. Cousin didn't know what to expect at the gateway, but they definitely weren't expecting no slave quarters.

"You coming?" Hermana shoves her machete into Cousin's hand. Her expression reminds Cousin of their mother, of a slyness, as Hermana turns her back and walks into the darkness.

There are photos in a shoebox in the room where Aunty and Papa Baker sleep. People with Cousin's jawline or Cousin's forehead or even wearing Cousin's old blue-black baseball cap that was sent to Jamaica, as if there was a line up from people on the island who desperately needed a blue-black baseball cap, are in the photo.

There is also a photo of Cousin and their mother, weathered and sepia. She has a hand on her hip and the other on the grill in front of a veranda with a small child peekabooing between her legs, face blurred. On the back, in fine blue ink from the hand of someone who has written many letters in cursive, reads: *Yvonne and child, Spanish Town*. Cousin would commit this photo to memory, the expression of their mother in a place Cousin doesn't remember ever visiting.

In that moment, against the darkness, if you strip that photo down to just the face, Hermana is Yvonne's perfect replica.

"You coming?"

° ◎ °

THERE IS A TRICK to farming in the dark.

An inherited skill to gather light to work the soil so late. A stamina for summoning strength after a double shift, so to speak. The gumption to exercise a choice to grow a crop. Pride in having your own tools. The ability to sound out uncensored labour (whistling, humming, pausing, laughing, singing to the plants) without repercussions. When pockets of liberation are so miniscule, near invisible, Hermana and others found ways to night-farm.

The soil is cooler in the evening—best time for watering—a tin can or old gourd will do, to clap the earth wet. Crickets are heard skyward and jackals cackle far but clear over distant hilltops. Both croon against the rhythm of the hoe: soil lines are marked and parted, the scalp of the earth sectioned and seeded. Like this here head, the tuff land stay tuff. How could Cousin know that this was the origin of the market? Perhaps that's why the portal drew them here to show them in the first place. All that's certain is that Hermana knows the trick.

Perhaps it was inevitable to cross the threshold, despite being terrified every time to do so before. Even think so before. It's as if the inklings of a phantom-hurricane jolted Cousin's nervous system the moment they stepped forward, one foot after another, away from the convenience store basement and toward the moonlight by the rocky cliffside.

And no, Cousin never dead. But something shifts. The cane cutters' children feel it. A heavy rain pummels the figures standing in the dirt instantly. But no one retreats. After all, it took years to turn the grounds, to convince the grounds to turn to soil. Not dirt. Not rock. Be soil! It tek long. Season after season. Hermana shared that not everyone survives long enough to see it through to harvest time. So no one left the battering storm, even as the torrent intensified.

"It would have come down anyway." Hermana smirks, not shielding herself from the downpour. "But now, you made it come quick. You and the next one." Despite the fact that a hurricane is shredding the clouds above them like ribbons, Cousin rests their hands on her shoulder, loosens their jaw. Cousin sees themself in her stern lip.

"You think you're the first to find this portal?"

Hermana isn't raising her voice when she says this, but the bass in her register shakes Cousin all the same.

"Huh, you think you're the first?"

"I did, yeah," Cousin admits, "until now." The wind makes playthings of their locs, whipping about against the darkening sky. Cousin squints as dust and debris dance between the two, and over their shoulder stands Cuz in the distance, edging from her own door-portal, the front of her throat long-arched and exposed. She is completely soaked.

"Well, you're not the first." Hermana shakes her head, unphased by the disaster overhead, as if she's outlived hundreds of hurricanes. And perhaps she had. To Cousin, she is as timeless as duppy, but she is blinking and solid and as warm-blooded as the two of them, as all the cane cutters' children who share a strange resemblance in some bizarre way to people in their bloodline.

Cuz stands in awe, her head back in terror as the storm grows in strength.

"We cyan stay 'ere."

Cousin notices Hermana's muscles, the result of countless hours of brutal labour. Cuz unlatches her gaze from the heavy sky, her afro unmoving, and meets Cousin's eyes with a message: *We muss truss har.*

Trees are plucked from the earth and their roots sweep the roofs of houses. Chaos churns the colours of the sky and eventually the winds silence all three youths momentarily.

Trust. Okay. Here goes.

○ ◎ ○

TONIGHT IS A not-so-good night. Vonnie works in the heat. Even in the cool of night, the air is still sweltering. Her mother Gladys used to tell her how her people from long-time-back-a-time used to farm in the evening. Not by choice. Maybe that's why she has sharp vision, even though she is aging everywhere else: in her back, in her knees, in her hips. But the thing is, Vonnie can make out precise shapes in the dark. Can parse out darkness of bush from darkness of night, darkness of skin from darkness of seas.

But tonight no good. Vonnie uses a small hand hoe and grows a few provisions, mainly things she can plant and water and eat with no fuss. Callaloo shot up quick this season but her arthritis won't allow her to strip the stalk. Last time it grew so bountiful, she had ribbons of green trash on her kitchen floor. She had just bought the property back then, three-four years ago now, and had been thinking to reverse-send for Cousin—a lie to herself. She didn't even tell Yvette she moved back to the island. Didn't want to start nothing. And Portmore is so far and Yvette rarely leaves St. Catherine and … and … they hadn't spoken in so long. What use is it to feign friendship with a twin-sister? Just because Vonnie homesick? Just because Vonnie fail at being an upstanding immigrant in both England and Canada? Just because Vonnie left her one and only pickney with her miserable older brother—"Lawd gawd, Yvonne, yuh just like Gladys." Tiring of mothering runs in the family. Sure, Yvette is ordinary, but damn that woman do love her pickney bad, all five, even the likkle one with no manners, the who favour Gladys bad, the one who can dance, byoi!

Does her own yuht dance? Don't make so painful a question, Vonnie. Three years is a long stretch fuh young people, and things aren't much better now. That's the thing about having a hard night, Vonnie can't hide from memory but she will damn well own her choices—at least as Vonnie. As Ms. Yvonne—that's what Cousin call her on the phone—it's not so clear as simply peering into the dark.

Proximity to knowing if her yuht can dance or cyan dance or if she's around long enough to teach them fuh dance doesn't feels like Vonnie's problem. Another set of skin. She keeps peeling it away, and it keeps growing back. The only regeneration she's interested in is her garlic this rainy season. Call Baker soon, she keeps saying to herself. But the pickney is clothed and fed. Is attending nice Canadian schools, which is better than what she can provide for them here.

Her ears start ringing as if to call bullshit. A terrible piercing sound. Vonnie tries to shake it off, her locs are pinned in a hive to keep out her face, but some shake loose. Hmph. Baker send some photos on WhatsApp, and Cousin is growing out their locs too, "like dey mumma." Stop, nuh! It's this headache and the air pressure and the heat and this day turn funny. First, she misplaces her tools and earlier she was fighting wasps when she stepped on a nest. Clumsy and dangerous. *Lawd gawd, Yvonne!*

Most time night-farming allows her to forget, but evenings like this one, when the moon can't decide if it is wrapping itself in cloud or not, stories eke out of the body from the labour. Vonnie takes a moment from the work, leans her big shape against the strength of a breadfruit tree. The leaves flutter and cut through the hard memories. Vonnie has been holding her breath and finally releases.

Her solitude is never a mistake.

Successfully relying on the ways she relates to plants instead of her failed attempts at relating to people is never a mistake. This may be all she can do today, she concludes. Her bed, a humble mattress tented by a mosquito mesh, isn't calling her just yet but the day was long. She grows tired. Her rough hands grip the round bark of the tree and Vonnie soon picks up her tools she discerns in the soil. She brings them to the shed, the half-lean shelter with paint-peel that is related to blue and grey.

She's been known to have miscalculated the width of a door before, an embarrassing confession where she can laugh at herself for not quite squeezing through a too-small opening. *Yuh have no business passing t'ru this one*, but also the joy of aging means you shed the memories, welcome forgetting, lose the weight. In the quiet, tonight especially, that is not the case.

The door of the shed has grown. Wide. Transmuted somehow when she wasn't looking, a differing appearance only she notices. The winds pick up, harsh and sporadic. Massive boulder-of-breadfruit pelt the earth from on high, nearly clotting Yvonne. The door, it widens yes, but there's also a violent rumble. And a deep, hard glow pulsating through the cracks. The rumbles persist, as if the knock from an army awaits her. As if the pestilence of cholera could seep through. As if the turbulence from a hurricane is behind the door. As if the face she's been avoiding could answer, looking for answers.

PAROXYSM

Zalika Reid-Benta

OIZYS ALWAYS ASSUMED THAT if she ever contracted the virus, laughter would be what killed her. Janus, a man in her building, on her floor, had died that way. The hall had echoed with his death. Every night, she could hear it through the walls—his raspy, wheezy, uncontrollable laughing. Even when he screamed in pain and cried out for his mother. Even when he pleaded to live, he laughed loudly and forcefully. And then he was quiet. It was quiet.

To Oizys, having no choice but to laugh at the decay of your own body because the sickness—the paroxysm—attached itself to your cells, to your biology, to your being, was the most gruesome way to go. It made sense to her, then, that that would be how she did go. No one got to choose which emotion, or expression, would be their executioner. If she could choose though, she'd choose something appropriate, like sobbing or yelling, any outburst of anger. But life was full of ironies, and she saw no reason why death would be any different, and that brought her back to laughter.

No one knew how the paroxysm formed or what it meant, only that its first known case began when, nearly a year ago, a woman started screaming on the Yonge subway platform after a significant train delay. She hadn't stopped screaming when the police came or when the paramedics came or when they committed her to the hospital. She hadn't stopped even when they'd reversed her sedation. When she'd died weeks later, there were already dozens of other cases—mass hysteria in the streets, in offices, in hospitals—and Oizys had decided to shut herself away.

•

IT ONLY TOOK THREE days for the stench in the apartment to become unbearable. Oizys thought she would have at least another forty-eight hours before action had to be taken. That had usually been the case. The garbage bags were piled by the door, bulky with old food and takeout containers and Kleenex boxes. They were five high and tightly tied; every time one had filled up, she'd double-knotted it in an attempt to minimize the stink since she knew she wouldn't throw the trash out immediately. Six bags were the limit. One week, it had been seven.

She would have to go at night. Morning, really. Two

a.m., maybe three, if she could wait that long. The chances of seeing a neighbour on the way to the chute were slim then, especially since it was Wednesday and the tenants her age were studying or working or sleeping and not tipsy and partying and giggling in the halls or blasting music, like they did on Saturdays at that time. On the small chance that she did see a neighbour, she'd do what she always did in such rare instances, turn around and run back into her own apartment.

The door she needed was forty steps from her own. She'd counted once. It would be quick. Painless. It always was. After all, it was just walking. *It's just walking, it's just walking, it's just walking.* She turned those words over and over in her mind, both as encouragement and a kind of self-admonishment. She wasn't on the train. At a restaurant. She didn't have to brave hordes of people in a mall, any one of them a potential host and a potential trigger to the paroxysm that rendered its victims agonized in fits of coughing or sobbing or screaming or hyperventilating until exhaustion took over and they became sluggish and disoriented and then, finally, catatonic. It was her own hallway. No real, imminent danger.

At 3:30 a.m., Oizys looked out her peephole, pressed her ear to the door. The floor was shrouded in sleepy silence. The mechanical click of her turning the lock and the metallic squeak of hinges when she opened her door a crack seemed to echo for everyone to hear. There was no better time to leave.

Oizys wanted to creep to her destination, make a light-toed excursion of the forty steps she had to take, but the bags were too heavy for anything other than a lumber. When buying them online, she had clicked on the box that said extra-large, and she'd stuffed the bags full until they were nearly overflowing with egg cartons and paper towel rolls and collected dirt and dust from the vacuum when she'd mustered the energy to clean. Tonight, she lined them outside her apartment door and then she hauled them, one by one, to her destination, sometimes hitching a bag over her shoulder like a Santa Clause of shit. She pushed the bloated plastic down the chute, using her hands and elbows to force them to fit through the rather unforgiving square opening.

Back inside, she let out a breath she didn't realize she'd been holding and tried not to panic at the thundering of her heartbeat. Inhale. Exhale. *Breathe.* Calm. Sure, there wasn't exactly a correlation between a racing pulse and paroxysm, but it'd been concluded that emotional stress—resentment, irritation, anger—triggered the virus. Oizys thought of the slurred chants she always heard through the walls on Saturday nights:

Out-party paroxysm!

The finance bro down the hall was one of those people who threw Dopamine Parties as a preventive measure—as a way to "create a safe, non-confrontational space to elevate moods, promote pleasure and happiness, to bring down the negativity that feeds paroxysm." He said that he threw the parties in honour of Janus, but Oizys just thought it was an excuse for debauchery and did more to spread the risk of exposure than counteract it. Using Janus's name was just in bad taste.

She looked at her foyer and felt something in between relief and satisfaction at seeing evidence of her accomplishment—a clear space that was desperately needed amid the delivery boxes and the bins of canned food she stocked "just in case," and the packs of toilet paper and paper towel and Kleenex boxes. She smiled. The clearing reminded her of how big her apartment could be. Clear space for a clear mind.

Later, she woke before her alarm. It wasn't because she'd forgotten to pull down her blinds and her bedroom had brightened with the morning sun. It wasn't the barking—well, yapping—she could hear from either the dog upstairs or the one next door. It was the stench. The same stench from the garbage. It had lingered.

Oizys groaned. She'd been strategic with the placement of the bags. The ones containing anything viscous like syrup, or anything liquid like the last sips of orange juice left in a bottle, she'd stacked at the top of the small heap, so any leakage would ooze onto the trash below and she wouldn't have to clean anything. There should be no residue on her floors. The smell should've gone with the garbage. She walked into her living room, expecting to see sticky spots or leftover grease on the laminate wood, but instead found the same number of garbage bags heaped together in the same spot she had cleared only a few hours earlier.

For a few long moments, she did nothing but stare. It was all she could do. Reconciling the reality of what was in front of her with the inconvenient detail that such a reality was, in fact, impossible, proved a challenging exercise that physically hurt her head. She had taken out all the trash. She hadn't imagined it. She hadn't somehow miscalculated the number of bags that needed to be thrown out. Wildly, she wondered if someone had broken in when she was asleep and put them there. Why someone would come into her apartment just to leave trash bags, she didn't know.

Or maybe, she was imagining the bags now. Maybe she was dreaming. That seemed more plausible. She had read an article about a woman who, when she'd dreamed, had been living this amazing parallel life, and when she'd woken up, she'd been so sure that her reality was the dream, only to fall into a depression when she'd accepted the truth and realized that her dream life was more fulfilling than her actual one. Though, if this were Oizys's parallel life, it seemed like a waste. Paroxysm still existed, everything was exactly the same, except that the multiplying garbage bags would be some kind of glitch.

First, Oizys tried to snap herself out of a dream she wasn't even sure she was having; she yelled, she told herself to wake up, she blinked rapidly. Then, she untied each bag and wrinkled her nose at the distinct but equally rancid reek each bag released when opened. Rotten food from the kitchen. Old menstrual napkins from the bathroom. These were real. Tactile. Stubbornly material. Then, in the space of a blink, the bags multiplied. Five more. Bigger. Smellier. Piled next to the original mound. Oizys scrambled backward into the breakfast bar, knocking over half a dozen boxes of Kraft Dinner. Suddenly, there was yet another pile of garbage bags.

She started to feel lightheaded with terrified confusion. Was this a symptom of paroxysm that no one spoke about? Was this a new indicator of the virus? The list grew every couple of weeks. Did she contract it and not know? Oizys couldn't see how. Nothing about her routine had changed; she hadn't gone outside in twenty-one days, not even to check the mail, not even to buy food. She had groceries delivered to and left at her door, and all of her communications were electronic, so there was no need to go downstairs to the mailbox. The walls of her apartment had contained her entire world for months now. There would be no way to contract the virus. This was something else, something inexplicable.

She needed to talk to someone. Her phone was still in her bedroom, and the horrible thought that if she left, more bags would appear in her absence made Oizys debate whether or not she should go and get it. Reluctantly, she ran into her bedroom. Once she found her phone, she started typing a message to Lyssa.

This is going to sound weird and definitely more than a little ridiculous …

Then she remembered. Lyssa was sick, and Oizys was sure that while she wasn't a host, she had been Lyssa's trigger. She'd abandoned her at a movie theatre a couple of months before. For weeks before that, Oizys hadn't taken up her offers to go to any fetes, any Dopamine Parties, any brunch dates, anything where there would be people.

I'm your friend and I'm just worried about you being alone for so long.

Oizys had insisted that safety was not, in fact, in numbers with her texts back.

Did you watch the news? Look at Health Canada? Paroxysm spreads through contact.

There was the experiential evidence too that seemed to suggest that paroxysm only activated in public or in places with other people.

It's scientifically proven that socializing releases endorphins and that dopamine levels are higher overall when humans interact, she'd countered. *You need to get out more! We can do something small. A movie. The one a few blocks from your place. A matinee.*

Theatres had limited audiences to about twenty people, and less than half that many would be in seats on a Monday afternoon.

You can still have a life and be safe. You're letting this thing run you.

Oizys agreed. That day, she had made it out of the apartment. She had even made it most of the way to the theatre. Lyssa had been outside and brightened when she saw her waiting for the traffic light to turn green across the street, but once it did, Oizys was suddenly overcome with the feeling of impending doom. Something was going to go wrong in that theatre, she knew it. Her chest started to flutter unpleasantly, and the thought of panicking in public, of risking exposure, made Oizys turn around and walk back to her apartment without a word. Her phone had vibrated with a confused text.

Hey, where are you going?

Oizys?

And then an angry one had followed.

Oizys, what the fuck??

Once she'd made it back to her apartment, Oizys forced herself to calm down and take deep, almost luxurious breaths in and out. Then, she'd responded, *I just can't. Sorry.*

Lyssa had fallen ill an hour or so later in the middle of the movie. Her paroxysm was rageful screaming. Oizys messaged when she'd found out. Insufficient words like *Sorry* and *How are you feeling?* and *They're getting closer and closer to a cure*, when what she had really wanted to say was *I'm so sorry about the movies* and *Do you blame me?* and *I wouldn't be mad if you wished me dead.* There hadn't been any responses, but Oizys chose to believe that the silence was out of anger and not because there wasn't anyone to send a reply.

Oizys deleted her text to Lyssa and tried to think of who she could contact, who hadn't phased her out of their lives when she'd continued to deny invitations to do things outside. If she texted her parents, they would want to speak on the phone or video chat with her, and Oizys had been adamant in her refusal to do either, save for fifteen minutes on the last day of every month.

Seeing the faces and hearing the voices of people she knew felt too risky for her; it could cause emotional responses too unpredictable to track. One shift in expression, one change of tone could tinge joy with a vague sorrow, could create an undercurrent of resentment in an expression of gratitude. The complexities of human contact left one too vulnerable to the triggers of paroxysm. And so Oizys did without.

In fact, it was better not to text anyone, she decided. It would cause worry or confusion or unease—all things best avoided to stay safe and healthy—and Oizys wanted no more lives on her conscience. She put her phone in a desk drawer and went back out into the living room.

The stench made her choke. In the few minutes she'd been in the bedroom, the garbage bags had multiplied at least another five times, and Oizys could no longer control her panic. This was some sort of haunting, some sort of karma, some sort of punishment for a past indiscretion. What other possibility could there be? Once again, she thought of telling someone—she thought of sending them a recording so they could see how she was plagued—and once again, the thought of being a burden or being a trigger kept her silent.

Instead, she decided she would simply brave the hallway

in the afternoon hours. Two by two, she dragged the garbage bags to the chute. Heaving. Hauling. Pushing. Heaving. Hauling. Pushing. After a few minutes, she realized her efforts were futile. For each bag she threw out, more simply appeared in its place.

Oizys was shaking. She covered her mouth with her hand in shock or puzzlement. "There has to be something I can do," she muttered to herself. "Something."

For days, she did everything she could think of doing: she opened all of her windows and sprayed air freshener for the stink that, after a while, became the standard smell of her apartment; she put the garbage bags on the balcony; she continued to push them down the chute. She stayed as active as she could in ridding herself of the bags so the powerlessness nagging at the back of her mind wouldn't spiral into a trigger for the virus. But the bags never stopped appearing and then multiplying, and soon they filled her entire living room.

Her parents would send texts, and she'd reply, as if everything was normal. She took selfies for her updates to them, all smiles, all positivity.

See some garbage bags in your picture, hon. Don't let the housework get away from you.

I'm working on it.

A clean living space brings about a clean headspace.

Yep, I got it!

Clear space for a clear mind.

I'm fine.

But the bags were encroaching upon her. Trapping her. Mocking her. They kept her from sleeping, they kept her from eating. Soon, she was sure, they would keep her from breathing. They were piling on top of each other now that they'd covered the floor of the living room.

They almost reached her TV, which she always kept on and turned to the news. Paroxysm cases were getting lower, apparently. There was an experimental drug. On her phone, she watched an influencer collapse into a fit of giggles on Live; another one pranked their viewers with primal screaming—comments called for their apology, for their head, for an actual Paroxysm diagnosis to debilitate them for real; she watched recordings of Dopamine Parties, of wellness retreats.

The bags kept coming.

"Why are you doing this?" she yelled at the different piles one night. "What do you want? What do you want from me?"

Sometimes, when her neighbours passed by, or when attendees of the Dopamine Parties made their way to the apartment down the hall, she could hear them remark on the odour that lingered in the hall. She should wrench open the door and show them the bizarreness of her reality, the never-ending river of garbage she had no choice but to swim in.

What she should actually do, she thought, was leave. Just leave. Go to her parents' house. Go to a hotel. Go somewhere. Anywhere that wasn't her apartment. It was easy. It was so easy. And yet it couldn't be done. What if she left and then once she came back, the bags had taken over her entire apartment? What if the garbage bags followed her and she doomed someone else to her fate?

One night, Oizys tore into the bags. She kneeled on the floor and ripped open the plastic, and as if spilling out from a belly, dirty tissues and old chicken bones and rotten vegetables and food-stained milk cartons poured out in stinking heaps. Oizys kept tearing and digging, searching for an answer or a clue, searching for any sort of reason in the orange peels and the pop bottles and the dirty rags, until she stopped slashing and looking and started to sob. Even when she'd gotten a text from Lyssa—*Took that drug. I'm getting better*—she kept sobbing.

JUST SAY GARUKA

Aline-Mwezi Niyonsenga

IT WAS MY FIRST and last summer in Saskatoon. I realized I could walk long distances without feeling tired. From my street on the east end, I walked all the way to the riverside, where the trail was both gravel and soft sand. Bushes and reeds obscured most of the view of the river and other paths downhill. I'd gotten bored with the roundabout trail my dad had shown me to get close to the river, so I pushed aside some reeds and found there was a more straightforward path. After some slipping and sliding on trampled grass, my foot almost getting stuck in a moment of mud, I arrived at a spot where the river was shallow and deceptively docile, running clear and sparkling under the same sun that had mocked us in winter not two months ago. It was there I heard a thud and turned in time to see a girl my age and with my skin tone rubbing her butt while a carpet floated above her head.

"Wait, what?" I must have said this aloud because both carpet and girl jumped a few feet in the air and settled flat on the ground.

"Oh no," she moaned. "Could you keep a secret?"

I smiled. "Sure." Secrets made friends and I hadn't made any this year.

Too bad it was my last year.

•

HER NAME IS AKALIZA. Mine is Sophie-Ange. We didn't talk about it, but it's clear our parents are from the same country. They're just clearly not in the same friendship groups. I brought beignets to our second meeting.

"Ooh, amandazi! Thank you."

Not mandazi, amandazi. That confirmed it. Akaliza stretched before mounting on the carpet, an ordinary Turkish or Persian rug with red-and-gold designs.

"How come you can fly on a magic carpet?"

"Oh, my mom is from a region called—" She coughed on a piece of beignet. I handed her some water and waited for it to pass. "—so flying is an art I learned from my grandmother."

"If you can fly, why are you using a magic carpet?"

"It's like training wheels."

Watching her train was fascinating. And boring. First, she let the carpet hover for a bit and brought it down. Hover and bring it down. The effort made sweat drip past the edges of the scarf wrapped around her head. Akaliza always wore a scarf around her head. The day before it was streaked blue with black-and-white birds. That day it was orange with butterflies.

"Why do you wear a scarf around your head?" I asked.

"Pass me the water?" She chugged it down. "It's not because of the tignon laws."

Apparently, slaves and freed persons in New Orleans were forced to wear scarves around their heads because their curly hair was too distracting. But scarves are also great for protecting your hair, so Akaliza wears them year-round. I know she didn't learn any of this in school because at my school, Black History Month was a faded poster on a wall outside the teacher's lounge. Nothing was said. Nothing was done.

Akaliza sat on her carpet, closing her eyes until the carpet wobbled then floated. She inhaled to bring it up, exhaled to bring it down. Her torso shook with the effort. You need a lot of effort to fly a magic carpet.

I handed her another water bottle. There were three more packed in her backpack. "Wouldn't flying without a carpet be easier?"

"No, I'd have to manipulate the air to support me. Air has many currents and it's invisible." She crushed the empty plastic in her fist. "A carpet, I can see."

I started to bring books to her practices and lie back on an igitenge on the gravelly shore. It had a repeating dove motif between purple waves. Sometimes a pince-oreille scuttled onto it, somehow blending with the silver accents in the waves. I don't know what "pince-oreille" is in English.

Akaliza practiced every day except when she worked. She worked at McNally Robinson. I tried to apply for a job there but there weren't any openings. One day in June I took copies of my resumé on a walk to the nearest shopping centre. It was only me on the wide concrete sidewalk. Between each store was a long stretch of grey, and I knew this part of the city wasn't made for pedestrians. I stopped by Indigo, where they told me to apply online. Compared to Indigo, McNally is like a tumble of books in a treehouse. I'm pretty sure it has a treehouse display in the middle of it. I remember a giant tree. They told me they'd finished hiring. Later I realized June was too late to apply for a summer job. Not even Tim Hortons wanted me.

The space Akaliza and I shared was a bubble of warmth, surrounded by the occasional whizzing of dragonflies and the call of a bird. The reeds provided a wall, and the view across the river was often empty, an abandoned stretch of riverside that Akaliza must have picked on purpose. Sometimes people sat there, and I wondered if they could see us. I couldn't see their faces.

Akaliza shrugged when I asked her. "It's sunny and bright, right? Maybe they can't see. People come and go all the time. No one's ever cared."

When she tried to fly over the water, she hovered barely

a metre above the rippling surface. Maybe people thought she was trying to sail across.

•

ONE DAY AKALIZA CAME with a different carpet, a mat that seemed like it was made of tightly woven straw. "This is my grandmother's umusambi," she explained.

"What happened to the other carpet?"

"My mom figured out I was using it for practice."

"I thought she was teaching you?"

"No, my grandmother was. My mom wants me to fit in because she had to fit in."

I wonder if that's why my parents never properly taught me their language. I wonder if I'll become just like them in the next place we move to, obsessed with trying to fit in.

That day Akaliza managed to move about two metres out before splashing into the water. It was shallow enough that she managed to wade back to shore. I clutched my copy of *Binti*, worried. "Maybe practice on land more?"

"Don't worry." She shook out her gitenge pants. They're red and navy with green beetles all over them. "If it ever comes to that, there's a command for returns. Just say 'garuka' and I'll be back."

Garuka, garuka. I muttered it in my sleep, dreaming of near drownings and the ground splitting beneath my feet. It splintered away from the shore and set me adrift on the sea, away from everyone I've ever known.

•

I CAME TO SEE Akaliza practice every day except when I had a family outing. That summer we drove to the dinosaur valley in Alberta. I don't remember the dinosaurs, but I remember the reddish-brown canyon, and going across a bridge that could only support one car at a time. I told Akaliza all about it as she practiced going back and forth across the shore. "The trick is not to think about flying," she said. "Keep distracting me."

I told her the story of a million pince-oreilles covering the floor of our basement back in Magog, a throbbing silver mass that shifted as we cried from our spot on the futon across from the stairs. Akaliza did ten laps up and down the shore and told me they were probably silverfish.

Her goal was to fly her carpet across the river to the other side. She accomplished it one afternoon when I was halfway through *Binti*. A couple on canvas chairs with fishing lines clapped. She bowed and sat back on her carpet.

After two tries floating and crashing, Akaliza rolled up her umusambi and waved at me. The couple told her something that made her laugh. I waved back, rolled up my igitenge, and headed back home.

"What did the couple tell you?" I asked the next day.

"'Keep going! You'll get it.' It's like everyone I meet is rooting for me."

The couple also gave her tips on focusing on her breathing. Within the next two days, she was able to make round trips on her magic umusambi. I brought sambusa and we celebrated with Saskatoon berries and Crush cream soda. Akaliza insisted on calling it pop.

"Congratulations to our magic carpet queen!" I said.

"Thank you, thank you." Her face was radiant in the late-afternoon sun. It was somehow always golden hour when we met. Seeing her happy made me happy. Having a friend was great.

"This time I want to carry both of us across the river." she said.

"Can you do that?"

"Of course! It's the least I can do for all your support."

I wondered if now was a good time to mention she had a deadline.

•

I'D ASKED MY MOM about the region Akaliza was from and whether she knew people from there. Beans were cooking on the stove.

"A friend of a friend at school maybe," she'd said. "People from—" the pot hissed and popped and she reduced the flame "—they're known for travelling so fast it's like they're flying. Like they know how to fly on a magic carpet."

Akaliza and I still met every afternoon, and my parents were happy I was going outside rather than wasting away in the heat of our poorly insulated house. Boxes filled up the halls and living room. I'd packed most of my things and only books remained: the library ones and the ones I'd yet to read.

That afternoon Akaliza told me about how she loves this show called *Charmed*. It's about three sisters who find out they're witches and live in a big paid-for house in San Francisco.

"I want to be a cool witch like Prue, but my carpet flying is clumsy like Phoebe," Akaliza said. "My grandma didn't get the reference."

Akaliza also likes contemporary romance YA. She likes the kind where the main lead runs through an airport to confess their love to the main love interest. I lean toward sci-fi and fantasy. I like the ones where intergalactic journeys bring a band of misfits together and they travel off into the cosmos, together forever.

First, Akaliza practiced lifting the both of us on the umusambi. Sweat poured down her face. I wondered if I should cut back on my beignet intake.

"Ha!" she said in reply. "If I can't lift you, then it's my failure as a witch. My grandmother said people have been known to fly elephants on carpets, scaring poachers into avoiding them."

"Was she one of them?"

"I totally think she was."

I tried to picture her grandmother flying through Akagera National Park, elephant in the back.

"Is she …?" It's something I didn't know how to ask. I twisted grass between my fingers.

"Not here," she said. I didn't know if that meant dead or abroad. I don't think I can tell the difference.

Akaliza changed the subject. "Which school do you go to?"

A school in the east. She mentioned a Catholic school in the west.

"No wonder our parents don't know each other."

I didn't want to tell her it's because we had moved to the city recently. And we were soon moving away.

I switched subjects. "So you call yourself a witch. Aren't our parents scared of that word?"

"So?" Akaliza grinned. "I've watched enough *Charmed* and *Sabrina the Teenage Witch* to love it."

"My auntie loves that show. How old are you really?"

She rolled her eyes. "Sixteen."

"Same." I grinned, then thought about how sad it was. There were only two weeks left until I moved. Would Akaliza lift me up before then?

•

THE NEXT WEEK I got caught up in family gatherings and well-wishing parties. I realized I hadn't given Akaliza my contact details. It's usually the first thing you do as friends. Maybe I was afraid of getting close. Maybe it would defeat the purpose of keeping a secret. If I knew her details, I could use them against her.

We went to Regina, which is somehow flatter than

Saskatoon. My parents dragged us there to go to a barbecue at a friend of a friend of a friend's who was friends with our friends and wanted to wish us a safe journey. The greetings portion was awkward, as always, and felt like a pop quiz to check if I knew the language. There are so many greetings and possible responses to them that I always fail at the last one. If in doubt, say "yego" or maybe it's "nawe." I always say "yego" and get it wrong.

I awkwardly drifted toward the teens at the event, but they were all on their phones. I turned to the food table, eyeing ibigori, isombe, meat stew, and hot dogs. If in doubt, stuff your plate with food.

"Liza!" someone called.

There Akaliza was at the backyard gate, wearing her signature red-and-green gitenge pants. Her hair was in cornrows this time. In her hands was a deck of cards and an open invite for kids to join. Our eyes met and flitted away.

"I'm Sophie-Ange," I told the table. "Just Sophie is fine."

Someone whose name was either Jeremy or Jean snapped his fingers at me. "You're the family that's leaving right?"

I stared at my cards. "Yes."

As if to make it doubly clear, the hosts called my parents up and dragged me along with them. A pastor extended a prayer over our heads. When I looked up, I saw Akaliza look away.

NEXT TIME WE MET at the river, neither of us mentioned the party. Instead, we talked about each other. Akaliza was starting soccer in August. My arms can't coordinate around a volleyball. It was summer training at the moment in the lead-up to fall. There were no games to watch, or maybe Akaliza didn't tell me about them. I didn't ask.

Practice was our main focus, and we ate snacks in semi-silence. My stash of beignets was slowly dwindling because my mom couldn't take too much with us on the plane.

Not talking about me leaving felt more and more like waiting for the train to pass at a crossing. Once while in my mom's car, a train went back and forth over and over again. A line of cars formed on either side of the crossing, idling. The train went back and forth, back and forth for ten minutes, until the ding, ding, ding of the train crossing went off and the boom gates slowly lifted.

Akaliza started to bring beignets to replenish our stash. Sometimes the topic of a show we'd seen would come up and we'd laugh faintly, knowing we wouldn't be able to finish watching it together. Still, we huddled over a clip of Salem, the sassy talking cat from *Sabrina the Teenage Witch*, laughed, and went back to practicing. Akaliza would insist on watching an episode of *Charmed* and I'd imagine living in a big Victorian house in San Francisco with Akaliza and all the friends I'd made in scattered cities. Sitting on the carpet made me feel like dead weight while Akaliza strained against unseen forces to lift us up on her grandmother's umusambi.

A few days before my departure, she said she'd do it. The umusambi floated above the ground and glided over the water. I marvelled at the way the water sparkled in the afternoon sunlight but was too scared to touch it, for fear it would break Akaliza's concentration. I could hear her laboured breaths, great heaves. We slowly dipped until I could feel water slipping onto the carpet.

"Liza?" But she was already dropping her arms. We splashed into the water. My face hit the cold surface. It reminded me of the icy oceans of my dreams, the ones that ripped me away from every shore. Before I could let my nightmares play out, I ripped my head out and yelled, "Garuka!"

A flash of light against water and we were back on our familiar shore, half-soaked. I took one look at Akaliza. She looked back at me and sneezed. It was the cutest little *achoo* I'd heard, so I laughed and it was infectious, breaking the tension. Our laughter quickly turned to arm smacking over how the umusambi squeaked in its wetness. *Squeak, squeak!* The laughing stretched on until at some point we broke down into sobs.

Akaliza undid her scarf and used it to wipe her eyes. It was too wet to wipe anything. "I just wanted to carry you across before you left."

"You still have time."

"Why do you have to leave?"

I found napkins in my backpack. "I was happy to go, but now I want to stay."

We lay back on my igitenge, letting the sun dry us. The hems of my jeans were taking forever. Akaliza lifted one hand to the blue sky. Big fluffy clouds raced across its endless expanse. There's a reason why licence plates call Saskatchewan the land of the living skies.

"My grandmother died last year," Akaliza said. "I promised her I'd be able to fly before she passed. And then she went to the hospital—complications with diabetes." She sniffed. "I thought I had more time this time."

I took her hand and squeezed it. "Sorry for your loss. Mine passed away a while back." Last year actually. I didn't know her that well.

She squeezed my hand back. "When are you leaving?"

"The fifth."

She sat up and stretched out a pinkie. "I promise it'll happen before then. This is for my grandma, and my new friend."

I wrapped my pinkie with hers. "Keep in touch?"

"Yes!"

And that's how we finally exchanged numbers.

•

TWO DAYS LATER, WE met for the last time. It was a roasting thirty-five degrees Celsius, but that just meant no one could see us as Akaliza lifted us higher than she'd ever dared. This time I did look over the edge. We were a rippling shadow over sparkling water. The wind up where we were reduced the temperature by a pleasant breeze.

Akaliza adjusted our trajectory as we neared the shore. We cruised along the water's edge, enjoying a view of our secret place before it was replaced by reeds interrupted by gravel and sand. Our landing was more of a crash, tumbling on a grassy slump toward the shore. Akaliza lay back on the ground, chest heaving. I wiped her brow with a napkin. Several plastic bags of beignets lay in disarray. The bits of aluminum foil that wrapped around the sambusa I brought were strewn near the water. That's what I get for leaving my bag half-opened.

Akaliza managed to bring us to the part of the riverbank with the fancy old houses on the shore. If anyone saw us, they were pretending not to. Or maybe it was too hot out.

We unpacked sambusa and feasted on them with the last of my beignets and the endless supply of Saskatoon berries we both had. The inside of their plastic bags was stained red-purple where some berries had been crushed in the landing.

"Thank you," I said. "For being my friend to the very end. Thanks to you I got to see a new part of this place."

"Hey, we're still friends," she knocked my elbow. "And next time I'll fly all the way to you. Where are you going anyway?"

I told her.

"Wow! I'll try my best."

I chuckled. "It's okay. I have a command for returns. Just say 'garuka' and I'll be back."

ABOUT THE CONTRIBUTORS

Trynne Delaney
Trynne Delaney is a writer currently based in Tkaronto (Toronto) with deep roots in the Maritimes. They are the author of the poetic novella *the half-drowned*, winner of the Quebec Writers' Federation 2022 Concordia University First Book Prize, and the award-winning debut novel *A House Unsettled*. You can find more of their work at trynnedelaney.com.

francesca ekwuyasi
francesca ekwuyasi is a learner, storyteller, and multidisciplinary artist born in Lagos, Nigeria. Her debut novel, *Butter Honey Pig Bread* (Arsenal Pulp Press, 2020), won the Writers' Trust Dayne Ogilvie Prize for LGBTQ2S+ Emerging Writers. It was a finalist for a Lambda Literary Award, the Governor General's Literary Award for Fiction, and the

Amazon Canada First Novel Award, and was longlisted for the Scotiabank Giller Prize and the Dublin Literary Award. *Butter Honey Pig Bread* was also a contender for CBC's Canada Reads. Her short fiction, essays, and criticism have appeared in numerous publications. Her story "Fuck You, Money" will appear in the anthology *Be Gay, Do Crime* (Dzanc Books, 2025).

Whitney French
Whitney French (she/her) is a writer, educator, and publisher. She is the editor of the award-winning anthology *Black Writers Matter* (University of Regina, 2019) and *Griot: Six Writers' Sojourn into the Dark* (Penguin Random House, 2022). Her novel-in-verse, *Syncopation*, is forthcoming from Wolsak & Wynn Press in 2025. A certified arts educator and assistant professor in creative writing at the University of British Colombia, Whitney is also the co-founder and publisher of Hush Harbour, the only Black queer feminist press in Canada.

Aline-Mwezi Niyonsenga
Aline-Mwezi Niyonsenga is allergic to place. She writes about migrant experiences with the help of a tornado auntie, a lion goddess, a boy stuck in reflections, the occasional ghost, and dragon rights activists. Her work has been published in *Uncanny Magazine*, *GigaNotoSaurus* webzine, *Fantasy Magazine*, *Augur*, and *FIYAH: Magazine of Black Speculative Fiction*, among others. It has also appeared in

anthologies such as *Africa Risen* and *super / natural: art and fiction for the future*. You can find links to her works on her website: aline-mweziniyonsenga.com.

Chimedum Ohaegbu
Chimedum Ohaegbu resides in Moh'kinstsis, colonially known as Calgary, Alberta. A three-time Hugo Award winner, she is the managing editor of *ROOM*. Ohaegbu loves birds, insect facts, stage plays, and orchestral video-game music. Her work can be found in *Strange Horizons, Arc Poetry, Contemporary Verse 2, The Magazine of Fantasy and Science Fiction*, and *The Year's Best Dark Fantasy and Horror* (volume 3), among others. She is currently working on her first novel.

Suyi Davies Okungbowa
Suyi Davies Okungbowa is an award-winning author of fantasy and science fiction. His latest books include *Lost Ark Dreaming* (a 2024 Nebula Award finalist), *Warrior of the Wind* and *Son of the Storm* (the Nameless Republic epic fantasy trilogy), and *The Intergalactic Empire of Wakanda* (a Black Panther novel). He lives in Ontario, where he is a professor of creative writing at the University of Ottawa. Find him online at @suyidavies and SuyiAfterFive.com.

Chinelo Onwualu
Chinelo Onwualu is a Nigerian writer and editor living in Toronto. She co-hosts *Griots and Galaxies*, a podcast about

African speculative fiction and the people who write it. A graduate of the Clarion West Writers Workshop, she studied journalism at Syracuse University. *Ex Marginalia*, her collection of essays by writers of colour, is available now.

Lue Palmer

Lue Palmer is a journalist and writer of environmental and speculative fiction. A recipient of the Octavia E. Butler Memorial Scholarship, they have been published in Canada, the US, and the Caribbean. Their first novel, *The Hungry River*, is forthcoming.

Terese Mason Pierre

Terese Mason Pierre is a Toronto-based writer and editor whose work has appeared in *The Walrus*, *ROOM*, *Brick*, *Quill & Quire*, *Uncanny Magazine*, and *Fantasy Magazine*, among others. One of ten winners of the Writers' Trust McClelland & Stewart Journey Prize, she was named a Writers' Trust Rising Star. Terese Mason Pierre is an editor at *Augur*, a Canadian journal of speculative literature, and the author of *Myth* (House of Anansi), a collection of poetry.

Zalika Reid-Benta

Zalika Reid-Benta is a Canadian author. Her debut novel, *River Mumma*, was shortlisted for the 2024 Trillium Book Award and is an Amazon books editors' pick for Best Science Fiction and Fantasy. It was listed as one of the best fiction titles of 2023 by numerous platforms including CBC Books and *The Walrus*. Her debut short story collection, *Frying Plantain*, won the Danuta Gleed Literary Award and the Rakuten Kobo Emerging Writer Prize for Literary Fiction. It was shortlisted for numerous awards, including the Toronto Book Award, the Trillium Book Award, the White Pine Award, and the Evergreen Award. Her picture book, *The Twelve Days of Jamaican Christmas*, will be published in 2026.

TERESE MASON PIERRE is a Toronto-based writer and editor whose work has appeared in *The Walrus*, *ROOM*, *Brick*, *Quill & Quire*, *Uncanny Magazine*, and *Fantasy Magazine*, among others. One of ten winners of the Writers' Trust McClelland & Stewart Journey Prize, she was named a Writers' Trust Rising Star. Terese Mason Pierre is an editor at *Augur*, a Canadian journal of speculative literature, and the author of *Myth* (House of Anansi), a collection of poetry.